About the author

Emma Cox is Head of English at an independent school in Devon and also works as a 'gifted and talented' associate lecturer at Exeter University. Being creative is a lifelong love for Emma. She has been writing since the age of four and spends every weekend and school holiday creating new stories. *Malkin Moonlight* is her first novel.

malkinmoonlight.com
@emmaexeter

EMMA COX

Illustrated by Rohan Eason

BLOOMSBURY

LONDON OXFORD NEW YORK NEW DELHI SYDNEY

Bloomsbury Publishing, London, Oxford, New York, New Delhi and Sydney

First published in Great Britain in July 2016 by Bloomsbury Publishing Plc
50 Bedford Square, London WC1B 3DP

www.bloomsbury.com

BLOOMSBURY is a registered trademark of Bloomsbury Publishing Plc

A CIP catalogue record for this book is available from the British Library

ISBN 978 1 4088 7084 6

Typeset by RefineCatch Limited, Bungay, Suffolk
Printed and bound in Great Britain by CPI Group (UK) Ltd, Croydon CR0 4YY

1 3 5 7 9 10 8 6 4 2

this one's for you, mama

Chapter 1
Malkin Moonlight

Every journey starts with one paw step, and it is that paw step that the little black cat takes.

He takes it and finds himself on the soft ground at the edge of a riverbank. Freezing wet and soaking cold, he drags himself through the reeds and into a clearing lit by the light of the moon.

'Oh,' the little black cat says, blinking at the full moon's beauty.

The moon looks down at him, barely more than a kitten, standing proudly in the pool of her light. His little body is shivering, but his huge tail is held high and his sharp green eyes are shining.

'Tell me your story, little cat,' she says, and her voice is kind.

The cat flattens wet ears to his head and pushes his nose towards the magic of the moon-pull.

1

The stars stop their music to listen.

'I fear I wasn't meant to be born, oh Moon. I was taken from my mother when I was very small. I can just remember her face and sometimes I see her in my dreams. The Owners carried me and my sister and brothers into a barn where it was cold. The first week the rats were bigger

than us, and we had to stand in a circle to make sure they couldn't snatch any of us away. We missed our mother and sometimes we heard her voice crying for us, but we couldn't go outside the barn; we were kept locked in. My brothers and sister didn't mind, yet something inside me was pulling me to go out. I had a feeling that we needed to escape. But the door was always locked. Until tonight.'

'What happened tonight, little black cat?'

'The man Owner came into the barn and caught us playing games with the rats. He said it was not our job to play, it was our job to catch, and we were getting too big to feed. He grabbed my sister first and put her in a bag. I jumped in to save her, but he picked up the bag and held it tight, so we couldn't climb back out. We were trapped. Then he caught my brothers. One minute we were all crushed up together, and my sister was crying, and it was dark and hard to breathe, and we were pushing with all our paws. The next it was worse: water was coming in; I hate getting wet. I managed to tear a hole with my sharp claws and fight my way out. I can't swim, but I managed to step on to a crate that sailed me downriver, and here I am.'

'Here you are, cat. Despite all the odds.'

'It was I who made friends with the rats, Moon. When we grew bigger, and we were no longer afraid. I was the

3

one who made friends with them, and now my sister and brothers have been thrown away. I didn't know that I shouldn't. It's my fault we were thrown in the river.'

'No, little cat, it is not your fault. It happened because of your unkind Owner.'

'And I have lost one of my nine lives tonight. I lost it in the reedbeds. And I have lost my home and my family.'

'But soon things will get better. You will lead many special lives.'

'Do you really think so, Moon?'

'Oh yes, little cat, for I see great things inside you.'

'Me?'

'Do you not feel them yourself?'

'I just feel so cold and hungry.'

'There is a kindness inside you, little cat, and peace. It is like the peace I feel when I sail at my fullest. You will be brave, even when those around you are afraid. And you will make great sacrifices for friendship – you will be a true friend, like I am to the stars in my night sky. We are inseparable, through time and space.'

'But I am alone.'

'No journey is easy all the way, but your sixth sense shines so brightly it will guide you to your home, and it will help you in times of danger.'

'Even now my sixth sense is pulling me away, oh Moon. It is pulling me to a place down the river.'

'It will tell you the way to go. It will pull you, like I pull the tides, and it will guide you, like my stars do the sailors. You must heed its pull. It will be the tug of destiny. It will be important, not just for you, but for other creatures too.'

'But I don't even know who I am. No one has given me a name.'

'Then kneel down, little cat, for I have your name.'

The cat kneels on the grass. 'Please tell me my name, oh Moon,' he says, holding his head upright, his eyes full of her reflection.

'Close your eyes, little black cat, and I shall.'

He does and, as the moon moves directly over him, the little cat feels something wonderful racing along the paths of his blood and his sinews, and curling softly through his ears and tail, and tingling all along his whiskers, and finally ending deep inside his heart.

'Your name is Malkin Moonlight. I name you for myself, and here is your gift. Lower your head.'

Malkin Moonlight bends his head and presses his cold nose into the wet riverbank, and the moon lights the fur at the ruff of his neck with a white ring all around,

5

so that he will always have the protection of the full moon about him.

Malkin is filled with the sensation that comes from being defined for the first time. *So this is me. I am this.* *My name is Malkin Moonlight.*

Then, in the second that follows, he feels the curiosity and wonder of being given a present. 'Thank you, oh Moon,' he says, shaking his head and feeling the moonbeam circle around his neck. He rises to his feet and drops a tiny bow that makes the moon brim with pride for the little black cat.

'May your eyes ever be bright, Malkin, and your spirit pure, good deeds to do for cat-kind and for all.'

'I will, oh Moon, I will always do my best. Whatever my best can be.'

'That is all any cat can do, Malkin Moonlight. Follow your heart; it will help you find friends. Let your sixth sense guide you; your sixth will lead you to a home.'

'But what should my home be?'

'It should be full of love and kindness.'

'And Owners? Will there be Owners?'

'Not all cats need Owners, but they do need love.'

Malkin is about to ask the moon to explain more about love when she says, 'Goodnight. Dawn is coming.

It is time for me to go, but I will see you again.'

'Thank you, Moon,' Malkin says, 'and goodnight.'

'Be lucky on your journey, Malkin Moonlight,' the moon says.

Malkin turns and sees the silver path of the river as it winds its way to the sea. It is beautiful now, and gentle. So he lifts his tail high, pushes his nose to the wind, turns all his senses up bright, and takes the next paw step of his journey.

Chapter 2
The East of India

Malkin walks through what is left of the night and into a beautiful dawn that spills its paintbox of colours on to the river. He keeps on, into the daylight, until he can go no further. Then he lies down and sleeps on the riverbank. A few times he wakes to find he is shivering with cold even though a late spring sun is shining and he is in her light, which is a brand new feeling for him.

The world is busy with people – he can hear their noises rising and falling, but they are not like the angry noises of his old Owners; these are noises that carry happiness. Sometimes Malkin will peer through the slits in the reeds and see people walking near him, down to the little boats that bob in the river with the bright flags that wave in the wind, but no one sees him, small as he is in the dark mud, except the dragonflies that hover and stare and the bees that drone.

Malkin is very hungry, and thirsty. At dusk he manages to lift his head enough to lap at a muddy puddle. He knows he must find food or he will lose another life here. But Malkin is too weak to move, so instead he falls into dreams.

In his dreams he sees his sister's face and her paw held out towards him. He remembers how he tried to save her from the angry river. In his dreams he mews and cries, mews and cries.

The humans, returning from their boats, do not hear him.

Humans are so bad at hearing.

Malkin wakes in the blackness of the night and smells a beautiful smell: the best smell he has ever smelled. He opens his eyes and finds there is something to eat. He noses it. It is crunchy on the outside and has a soft, gooey inside. He takes a bite of the gooey stuff. It is delicious: salty and sweet at the same time. It sparkles with silver, like the stars, and tastes like secrets. Malkin tries to eat it slowly, but he can't.

He gobbles it all up very quickly.

He feels it strengthening him.

Now is the time to move.

Malkin puts out a paw to take a step. It hurts. He pulls his body up and tries to stretch, but he feels hot and cold at the same time. There is a wall ahead of him, a long red wall that runs between the river and the land on the other side. It is not a high wall for a cat with a tail like his, and yet he finds himself unable to leap like he usually can. Still he knows he must climb the wall and so he does. It makes his head feel dizzy, whirly, like he felt in the bag, but he reaches the top and sees the world all around. He sees a building covered in red flowers and a sign that swings in the wind, and behind that he sees the sea. It is the wildest and widest thing he has ever seen and for a moment he thinks it cannot be true. The air smells sweetly salty, like the flavour of the food he just ate, and the rushing sound of the waves makes his ears twitch: it's good and bad at the same time.

Malkin knows he must reach the building with the flowers. He can feel his heart pulling him towards it. It must be a good place. A safe place. Perhaps it could be his home. But as he walks along the wall he gets another feeling. A curious feeling, prickling and tickling his fur and pulling the claws from all eighteen of his toes. His sixth sense turns bright white and rushes through his body with all the might of the angry river. A sharp feeling comes into his claws, and his back arches up into the shape of a bridge.

He is being watched.

His eyes flick, checking for silent movements, looking for surfaces to leap upon, for exits to take. Each muscle beneath his black fur is tight. His whiskers tingle and tremble, sensing the air around his face.

He will not lose another life, not tonight, he will not.

And then his sixth sense ebbs away like the tide. The hot and cold feeling returns and Malkin feels his brain become blurry and his body shaky and cold. In that instant Malkin knows he cannot outrun another cat. He knows he is too weak to fight, but still he is drawn towards the building, so he takes another step and another until he finds he has stopped. He spins to see if something is standing on his tail, but there is no one there, just his own great tail trailing like a wet flag. He looks up at the moon as the arch leaves his body: the spin has cost him, has put the dizziness in his brain, and his paws give up the scratch and claw and crumple beneath him.

The sea wind howls.

Malkin falls.

As Malkin falls he tries to use his tail for balance, but it is full of slump, his paws scuttle against the wall, scrabbling for something to cling to. They find some ivy which slows him for a moment, but still he hits the ground and feels the bright light of pain.

Then all is motionless, save for the sea wind that gently combs his fur; and all is silent, save for the steady creak and whine, creak and whine of the sign above his head.

Malkin moves into the place cats go when they are letting go of a life. Deep inside, he feels the life fading: the very worst feeling. But right behind it he feels his next life: a new him, a future him, arriving to take him to safety.

High above Malkin a pair of eyes blink. They watched him fall. They disappear, then appear again, blinking and thinking, blinking and thinking, in the darkness of the night.

A window is nosed up, a body is pressed low, then it is outside on a window box. A face is held to the sea wind; fur the colour of cream and smoke is pushed backwards.

Balancing is done along a window box full of red geraniums, a special leap is performed on to a sign that says 'The East of India', with a painting of a ship. A young cat, barely more than a kitten, makes her familiar way down the scaffolding that supports the side of her pub, where the old stones are crumbling, and she lands softly by the cat that fell.

She nudges him with her nose, then reaches for him with her senses. It is no good.

'Oh, this is *very* bad. Oh, this is *awful*,' she says. 'He has just lost a life. He needs my help before he loses another. Oh, what to do?'

The girl cat is afraid. Rain begins to fall in heavy drops that soak the fur and make the paws cold. The wind howls all around them. The girl cat knows of only one place the fallen cat will be safe and warm – in the cellar – but she doesn't like the smell of it. It smells bad: of time that has gone, and animal lives that have been lost. She is quite sure it is full of the largest spiders, and she is *not* a cat that chases spiders.

Then she looks at the cat that fell and steels herself.

She lowers herself through the trapdoor that leads to the cellar, stands on a wooden barrel and reaches up. As gently as she can, she pulls the sick cat by the loose fur on his neck. He slides and lands with a heavy-sounding bump, then makes soft sounds of sorrow as he is pulled into the underground darkness.

Chapter 3

Roux

Malkin wakes up feeling wonderful. There is warmth all around him, and he is in the half-dark, which cats love best because it is where their senses are keenest. He opens his eyes and sees a small, pink, upturned nose very close to his own. Then he sees wide eyes that are lit from inside with the palest green. Zigzags come down from the corners of the eyes and end in white fluff. Two paws rest on his own front paws.

Malkin has not seen a cat that looks like this before. She is the colour of cream and smoke. Her fur is longer than his, and softer looking. Around her neck she has a collar with a shiny circle that moves. She smells of wet grass and small flowers.

Malkin looks up and sees fingers of light falling from between the slats above him. He wonders if he has lost all nine lives and this is heaven.

14

He doesn't think he would mind too much if it is.

Then he feels around his senses and realises he is not dead, but remembers that he has lost another life.

He is down to seven.

Which is a shame.

But he recalls what the moon said: that he would live many special lives, and it is true; this life already feels very different from the last.

The green eyes blink, then the girl cat moves her paws away from his and sits up. He feels the absence of her warmth very suddenly, like when clouds block out the sun. He would like the paws back, but he doesn't say so.

'Good morning.' Her voice is soft. 'How are you feeling? Can you sit up?'

'Good morning. Much better, thank you.' Malkin sits up and faces the girl cat. 'Is it you who has helped me?'

'Yes. You lost a life last night. I didn't want you to freeze and lose all your lives. Then I noticed you had a cut on your paw, and I think it was giving you the shivers, so I put some stuff that stings on it. It seems to have worked.'

'Thank you,' says Malkin. His change in circumstances is so extreme he cannot quite get used to it: he's moved from freezing and wet to warm and dry in one night.

'Did you know you had a cut?'

'Everything hurt,' Malkin remembers. 'I didn't know about one cut.'

'Well, you look *much* better, and it is nice to meet you. My name is Roux, by the way, with an *x* at the end. Like crossed claws or how humans draw kisses on blackboards or make a finger-promise. But you don't *say* the *x*, you just think it. Look at my collar, if you can read.'

'I can't,' says Malkin, looking at the shiny disc in front of him.

'Never mind. Try to say it as I said it.'

'Roux.' Malkin's voice is tired and has a crack running through it. He coughs and tries again. 'Roux,' he says, in a stronger voice, thinking of the *x*, but holding it inside.

'*Perfect*. And you are?'

'I'm Malkin Moonlight.'

'That's a very grand name.'

'Your name sounds like it comes from another world.'

'No, no, this world; my Owner gave it to me. But she was born in another *country*, across the wide sea.'

'Another country?'

'My Owner is from France. Her name is Cecilia and her father is the chef in this pub. I chose her when she came to the house I was born in. I was born in a big white house here in Starcross-on-Sea. One day Cecilia arrived

16

with her father and I went up to her and I told her to choose me. Of course, she didn't understand my words, but she understood well enough. She picked me up and said, "This one, Papa, I choose this one." Then she began to stroke me. She didn't put me down until we were in the car.'

'Is she kind?'

'Of course. She is *very* kind, and she loves me very much. She has golden hair that curls around and around. She doesn't mind when I bat at it. Not *too* much. But sometimes she puts down my mouse and tells me to play

with that instead. It's extremely fast, but I am an *exceptional* runner. She has dark eyes that go deep and deeper, just like the sea, although she is kind and *never* angry. To be stroked by her is the very best feeling. In the evening she reads me a story then tucks me into my basket, while she goes to sleep. When night is dark I sneak out through the window, but I'm back by the morning, and I *never* go far. Just to the window box or the benches. I was at the window when you fell.'

Malkin looks at his paws. 'My Owners were not so kind.'

'Oh! But what did they do?'

'They put me and my brothers and sister in the river.'

'Oh dear me – that *is* awful.'

'Was it you who put the food outside, Roux?' Malkin asks, twitching the tip of his tail.

'It was. I heard you crying in the reedbeds, so I carried some food in my mouth.'

'I was crying?'

'Yes, so I came to see. Your eyes were closed and you were curled up very small, and I could see your heart beating. You were hot and cold so I put my paws around you to warm you until the chef came calling for me. Then I kept watch through my window.'

'Thank you,' says Malkin, thinking for a moment about

the soft fur of the girl cat wrapped around him. It fills him with so much warmth it almost washes away the cold of the river.

'It was the circle around your neck I saw first. It is the purest white. It was almost glowing.'

'Yes. The moon gave it to me.'

Roux blinks. 'The moon gave you a present?'

'Yes.'

Roux stares and stares at Malkin's circle, so close her nose is almost touching his fur. 'Well. That *is* special,' she says eventually. 'I would *love* a moon present. I have dreamed about receiving a moon present ever since I was a very small kitten, but of course the moon only gives presents to *very* special cats. It is incredibly rare. You *are* lucky. I imagine that she saw such great things inside you. I wonder what they can be.'

'I don't feel very special.'

'Oh, but you *must* be. Didn't your mother tell you about moon presents?'

Malkin shakes his head. 'I was taken away from my mother when I was very small.'

'Oh. Oh, that *is* a shame.'

Malkin is quiet and Roux sits for a moment in his silence.

'Well, I suppose you'll be heading home now you're better,' she says, looking carefully at a smoke and cream paw. 'Your friends will be missing you.'

'I have no home,' Malkin says quietly, 'and no friends.'

'*I* could be your friend.'

'Could you?'

'Of course. And this can be your home for now, until we find you a new one, if you don't mind sleeping in a cellar.'

Malkin considers that as long as he is close to Roux, he wouldn't mind it too much at all.

'Thank you,' he says. 'And would you please show me your home and all the things outside?'

'Oh yes! That will be such fun. I can teach you all about the world, if you would like me to.'

'I should like that very much.'

'How much do you know already?'

'Hardly anything. You can use your sixth to read me if you like.'

'If you're sure you don't mind.'

'Of course not.'

Roux stands very close to Malkin and closes her eyes.

Immediately, in her sixth sense, Roux can see the world that Malkin knows. She is surprised by what she sees, and by what she doesn't. The feeling of being newborn and having a mother is barely there. As a tiny kitten there is some fear. Later there is some chasing, quite a lot of balancing, but few smells and flavours. No fish, no cream. So few good feelings. No soft grass beneath the paws. No butterflies to catch and quite a lot of rats that he seems to be *friends* with. Then there is the sadness of separation and a paw that he *cannot* reach to grab hold of, no matter how hard he tries. Roux feels the sharp feeling in her claws and almost opens her eyes when she feels the terrible anger of the river, but then she feels the creamy calmness of the blessing of the moon. Then something deeper and stronger makes her feel light and bright all at once. It is something powerful, like the feeling she gets when she watches the sea from her window box, or when the night falls and she is called outside to stare at the full moon. Her sixth sense rides up high on the feeling, and it feels good, like running really fast, or taking a great big jump and landing well. There is bravery, and hope, and peace and friendship. There is something even stronger too. Very strong.

She opens her eyes.

Malkin has been watching her. Now his head droops. 'I don't know much, do I?'

'Oh, but I can see what the moon saw in you! I know why she gave you a present. You are *very* special, Malkin – you are good and kind and you are going to do something important. Oh, I wonder what it will be. But, for now, let me show you the wide world. Are you feeling well enough? Do you feel the pull to go outside and play? I don't like it in this cellar: it smells bad and there is a spider's web just above your head.'

'Oh yes, please – I can't wait to go outside. I would like to play outside the whole day.'

'Perfect! The sun is shining and it is a special weekend so many people will be coming to the pub. Everyone will be happy and there will be so much to do. You can warm your fur. You can look at the drawings on the blackboard. You can meet my Owner. She will stroke you. Don't you love being stroked?'

'I've never been stroked.'

'Never?'

Malkin shakes his head.

'But, Malkin, that's terrible. Come on, follow me. Do you think you can manage the jump up?'

Malkin checks his tail. The balance is back. 'Easy,' he says, looking at the light through the trapdoor.

'Then come on!'

And Roux jumps up and pushes open the trapdoor and leaps into the world outside, and a second later Malkin follows her, performing a magnificent leap and landing in the daylight of his third life.

Chapter 4

The Sea

The next second Malkin is following Roux up the scaffolding to have a good look at the world. He does a bit of balancing and has some high-up fun. He accidentally scratches the painting of the ship when practising swinging, then he lands next to Roux in a window box full of red flowers.

'Look, Malkin. Look how beautiful the world is.'

And it is.

Malkin points his nose to the faint sea wind that whispers secrets in his ears.

'Are you ready to learn about the world?' Roux asks.

'Yes, I am. How shall we begin?'

'We can watch the sea and listen to the tales it tells. Or we can turn that way and watch the boats on the river. *That* way is the river, and *that* way is the sea. I think we must be the luckiest cats in the world. We can sit up here this morning and I can teach you about everything that goes by. Then we can go down to the benches at lunch-time to make the humans happy, unless there's a *dog*. Some humans bring dogs with them.'

Something in the way Roux says *dog* made Malkin's sixth sense go prickly and the fur on his white circle stick straight out.

'I always go inside if there's danger. And I have to be back in the evening when my Owner goes to bed – for story time. I sneak out once she's asleep – although I'm never out *that* long. Except for last night when I was looking after you.'

Malkin likes the idea of spending day and night with Roux doing all the different things, but even so, something burns more brightly in him. 'Oh, but let's go down to the sea. I want to feel what it's like up close. I've never been to the sea. Please let's explore.'

'I've never been to the sea either.'

'Never been to the sea?' Malkin asks in surprise. 'When it's right –' he waves a paw – 'there.'

'Malkin, you need to understand that I'm a *Domestic*. I don't feel the need to go exploring the wide, wide world. I like my home and I *love* my Owner. I like my food and my basket. The fish here is very fresh. A man comes every day with a box. We can watch out for him from here. If I go to his ankles and cry he gives me a small fish; he saves them especially for me, he says. There's no reason why you can't try that too.'

'But aren't you curious to see the world?'

'This *is* my world. This is what I wanted to show you. I can teach you everything you need to know from this window box.'

'But don't you want to see more? Can't you feel the pull of adventure? I want to go over there, to the other side of the wall that stretches all around.'

'The sea scares me. That much water is … too much. I'm not brave enough to cross the seawall. My Owner would not like it if she could not find me. Let's play chase down there, under the benches. Today is the day they call Saturday. Humans *love* Saturday. My Owner says this Monday is a day called *May Day Bank Holiday* so the humans are very excited as they are not allowed to do any work, unless they work in the pub of course, and the children don't have to go to school. It will be fun and everyone will be happy. Look! Here's the chef now. I smell *tartine aux sardines*. It's what I left out for you last night. Did you like it? I think it's the most delicious thing in the whole world. Come down, come down.'

Malkin watches Roux scale the side of the building, then wind herself around the black and white checked trousers of a man who places a bowl on the ground. It sends tangy flavours to the sky and Malkin feels sudden hunger in his stomach.

A bell chimes, and some birds fly off the roof. Then a young girl with curly golden hair skips out of the pub and starts to run her hands over Roux's fur. Roux tilts her head into the girl's hand, and weaves her tail around the girl's ankles like ribbon.

Malkin stays in his high-up place, watching Roux and her Owner, until Roux lifts her face and calls for him. Then he sticks his tail in the air and balances down the building.

'Roux!' says the little girl, when Malkin arrives on the ground. 'You have a friend!'

Then Malkin feels the girl's hands on his fur, and for the first time ever he is being stroked. It feels like kindness, and warmth. It is everything that is good and gentle, and the very opposite of being in the bag. Malkin feels the purrs racing each other through his body and tickling inside his throat.

'Listen to you purring! But you're so thin and tiny. I see why you didn't eat all your *tartine* now, Roux – you were saving it for your friend. Wait, I'll ask Papa for some more.'

The little girl goes back inside the pub and Roux noses the bowl towards Malkin. 'It's for you,' she says. 'Eat it.'

'After you.'

'I've had mine.'

'Are you sure?'

'*Quite* sure. Do eat it.'

Malkin does, and it is the same taste as the food he ate on the riverbank: quite the most delicious flavour in the world.

Then the little girl is back, and the stroking is back, and the chef puts some more *tartine* in the bowl, and this time Roux and Malkin share it together, their noses touching. They are filled with such energy that they run around all the tables and benches chasing each other, and the little girl laughs, and Roux says, 'Come inside, see the kitchen,' and Malkin begins to follow Roux and her Owner into the pub, but the chef stands in front of them both and claps his hands.

'*Non*. Not inside,' he says. 'He cannot come in the pub, *ma chérie*, he is Wild. He might have the fleas.'

Roux stops still and looks back at Malkin. Malkin looks

at the chef's scuffed shoes. He feels the whirling feeling inside, and his face is hot.

'I may be Wild and not Domestic,' Malkin whispers, 'but I don't have fleas.'

'Of course you don't,' Roux says. 'You look like a *very* clean cat. Humans' senses are *extremely* poor.'

'I'll just … I'll go back to the cellar,' Malkin says, turning for the trapdoor.

'Wait!' says Roux.

Malkin turns back.

'I've changed my mind. We *can* explore.'

'Really?'

'Yes. I think I'll be safe with you, as long as you stay close. You can teach me exploring and I can teach you all the things I know from my Owner's stories.'

'Wonderful!' says Malkin.

'But not *too* far. Just to the top of the seawall. No further than that. It's *very* dangerous: you should know – you fell off it and lost a life.'

The two cats run together and scale the wall, and Malkin can sense Roux is afraid, but she reaches the top, where Malkin keeps close to her because he can feel the dizziness rising from her and she has flattened her ears all the way back.

'The sea, old chaps, this is the sea,' a seagull cries, riding an air current and swooping low over their heads. 'Gorgeous, isn't she?'

Malkin breathes in. 'She's beautiful.'

He turns sideways and looks at Roux and feels happiness lapping inside him. He sees that the mood of the sea today perfectly matches her pale green eyes.

Then the wind whips up and for the first time Roux feels the sea on her face: soft splashes reach up and hit her eyes and her whiskers, salt spray licks at her nose, but in a tiny way that she doesn't mind at all.

In fact, she finds it makes her laugh.

And Malkin finds that the sound of Roux laughing is his favourite sound in the whole world.

Chapter 5

Horatio

A week passes very happily for the two cats. Then, one morning, just as Malkin is dreaming about stretching into a new day, Roux shoots through the trapdoor and lands on a barrel.

'Morning!' she says.

Malkin opens one eye. 'Morning, Roux.'

'Oh, I *do* hate that you have to sleep in this mouldy old cellar while I have a warm basket,' she says, seeing a spider scuttle across the floor and lifting her tail up high.

'I don't mind,' Malkin says, and he really doesn't. He yawns and stretches. 'It feels very early.'

'Yes! It's sunrise. I thought we could go and watch the sea change colour.'

'Good idea!' says Malkin.

'Race you. I'm going first because you have the climbing advantage of that big tail of yours.' And with that

Roux bursts back through the trapdoor, followed closely by Malkin, and they race each other to the seawall, and Roux gets there first, but Malkin catches her on the climb up so they both arrive at the top together. They watch the golden ball of the sun rise higher and higher and the sea glister and turn gold.

Explore! the world calls to Malkin.

He feels the spring in his paws, and the smells in the air, and the sounds of the world all around, and he is filled with the rushing of movement, so that he does not want to be still, not for a second, not when there are more friends to be made and smells to find. Every bit of him longs to cry, *I'm coming, world!*

'Oh, please can we go over the wall today? Not far. Just so I can feel the sand beneath my paws. Please, Roux?'

It is the way he says *Roux* that makes her stand still for a moment and think. 'My Owner says that it is important to wait for your second thought, not just think your first. She says that flowers can turn to fruit, if you let them. She's read me stories about animals changing and plants growing and hungry caterpillars becoming butterflies if they eat the right sorts of things.'

'That sounds wonderful.'

'So perhaps today I *will* open my heart to change.' She smiles at Malkin as she sees how much it means to him, how strong the pull inside him is to explore. 'Yes,' she says, 'today is the day I will explore further. But *just* over the wall, into the sand. And don't run on ahead and leave me.'

'I won't. I promise.'

'Paw promise?'

'Paw promise.'

And they touch paws on it.

'After five?' she asks.

'Five,' he agrees.

They look at their front toes and Roux counts to five and Malkin takes a paw step, just one paw step, down the wall. Then his great tail is high and full of balance and soon both cats are running down the wall, unable to resist the call of gravity to the ground.

They jump into the scratchy tufts of grass at the bottom – scratchier than either has ever felt – and then run instinctively to where the damp sand is, and along its soft firmness, and turn with marvel to see that it keeps their paw prints in long lines behind them.

'It's wonderful, Malkin! It's so wonderful! I *love* exploring. Let's race towards those fishing boats!' Then

Roux is gone, running ahead, her laughter falling behind her. 'I can't believe it, Malkin! To chase along the sand racing the waves and to feel the wind in your fur! Faster than magic! This *is* life!'

This is life, Malkin thinks, trying to catch up with Roux. But things are so beautiful, so interesting, and there are so many sights and smells that Malkin pauses to investigate the things around him. He touches a paw against a piece of sparkling sea glass that reminds him of Roux's eyes, and watches the scuttling journey of the little crabs, and sniffs a strand of seaweed, and taps over a twisty white shell to look at its hidden beauty.

'Come on, Malkin!' Roux calls.

'Coming!' he replies, and begins to run towards where she is waiting.

Then, very suddenly, Malkin stops.

'What's the matter, Malkin? Why've you stopped?'

But Malkin doesn't reply, so Roux runs back to him and pats him with a paw. 'What is it?'

Malkin doesn't react. She stands on his tail, but still the silly cat is just standing there with a peculiar look on his face. Roux nibbles Malkin on an ear.

It is possible it was more of a bite.

'Ow!' he says.

'Why have you stopped, Malkin? I want to race.'

'I can hear something.'

'What do you hear?'

'It's a sad sound. Someone is hurt. Someone needs our help.'

'Where?'

'Don't you hear it?'

'No. I can only hear the waves and the rush of wind in my ears.'

'It's coming from over there – where the land curves round like a claw and the fishing boats are tied up close together. Come on.'

And the two cats head that way, jumping across the ropes that run in lines along the beach, until they see.

'Oh no,' says Roux.

A seagull is trapped under a long blue fishing net. The sounds he is making are very bad. When Malkin approaches the bird flaps his trapped wings and tries to move, but he can't.

'We will help you,' Malkin says. 'Keep still.'

'Thank you, old chap,' says the seagull. 'Came down for a bite of fish, you see. Partial to a bit o' fish I am. Saw one in the net. Then the fishermen dragged the net up the beach and I got tangled.'

'Help me lift it, Roux.'

The two cats try to lift the net with their paws, but the net is very long and the seagull is in the middle of it. He flaps and squawks but he cannot get out.

'Oh, it's making it worse,' says Roux.

'I think I'm done for, chaps. When the tide comes in I'm sure to drown.'

'Oh, *don't* say that,' says Roux, and there is fear in her voice.

'We will claw you out,' says Malkin.

'These nets are tough, old chap, and the tide is coming in.'

'Don't worry, my claws are sharp,' Malkin says, holding up a paw. Five very long, very sharp claws shoot out. 'Come on, Roux, we've no time to waste.'

So Roux begins to bite at the net, but Malkin sits still, hooks a claw through the net and one by one he slices through the thread, with a wonderful sound, until there is a hole that is just big enough for the seagull to squeeze through. He drags himself out, but still his foot is tangled up, and it is a horrible sight to see him pulling against it.

'Stay still,' says Roux, and, very gently, she untangles the net from the foot with her teeth.

The seagull lies still for a minute on top of the blue netting, quite exhausted, his wings spreadeagled about him. 'Thank you,' he says breathlessly.

'How are you feeling?' asks Roux.

'My feathers are a bit ruffled, but the wings still work,' he says, lifting them up and down. 'Horatio's the name.'

'I'm Roux and this is my friend Malkin.'

'Pleasure to meet you both. How can I ever repay your kindness?'

'There is no need to repay us,' Malkin says. 'You needed our help. It was the right thing to do. That's enough, isn't it, Roux?'

'Yes! It is a good feeling to help others,' Roux agrees.

'I will be forever in your debt. We seagulls have long memories, wide as the sky, vast as the sea. I will look out for you both. If there is ever anything you need ...'

'Well ...' Roux begins, thinking of the cellar, 'Malkin *does* need to find a home.' But as soon as the words are out on the wind, she feels sad at the thought of Malkin leaving.

The seagull turns his head sideways and studies Malkin. 'A home?'

'Yes. But not just yet,' Malkin says quickly. 'There was a pull inside me, like the boats in the harbour tugging against their ropes. I feel I belong somewhere else, but the pulling has stopped for now, although I think it will come back.'

Horatio lets out a squawk. 'Don't need to tell an old seafaring chap about the pull. The call of the sea cannot be denied. A home, you say. Right you are. There is a place where cats live that comes to mind. It's a place I visit a lot, but it is not without its troubles ... if ever you're ready to move on, let me know and I'll show you the way. Now, I think I feel better. Yes, the wings are working again and the sun is up. It's time for me to be off. But I will see you again. Goodbye, Roux, goodbye, Malkin, and thank you.'

The cats wave goodbye as the seagull takes to the sky. They watch him for a moment, then they turn and walk back towards the pub.

'Oh, Malkin, I was *so* afraid. I thought we wouldn't get him out. Thank goodness you have such sharp claws.'

'That felt so good, Roux! That felt right. As if helping others is exactly what I'm meant to be doing. Did you like exploring, Roux?'

'Oh yes, I liked it *very* much, but I wouldn't have been brave enough to come over to this side without you.'

'I think you would, Roux. I think you are braver than you know.'

'And I think *you* are cleverer than *you* know.'

'Only because you're teaching me.'

The cats walk on in silence.

'Malkin?'

'Yes, Roux?'

'You may have *very* sharp claws, but I think I'm faster than you.'

Malkin turns to look at Roux. Her eyes are glinting. 'That's not true! I just stopped to look at things.'

'Race you to the seawall then.'

'Hey, wait – you had a head start.'

Malkin's heart races as he chases after Roux. This is being a cat, he thinks. Truly, truly a cat, and everything a cat can be – and a cat can be many things; and nothing – nothing – beats this feeling of running and exploring and helping others. This is me, this is what I was born for. This is who I am.

Chapter 6
Reading

One hot afternoon, Malkin and Roux are sitting in a patch of sunlight under a bench eating the food that the humans are throwing at them in return for strokes.

'This is delicious,' says Malkin. 'I wonder what it is.'

Roux wanders over to the blackboard, and Malkin follows. She points her nose up at the words. 'Well, it's not mussels, because they are the things in the blue-black shells that you play with but won't eat. It's not quiche, because neither of us like that, and you *know* how you feel about salad. I think it must be the chef's special. It's definitely got fish in it and pastry and I think herbs.'

'You're so clever, Roux, being able to read.'

Roux flicks back her ears. 'It's my Owner who's the clever one: she reads to me every night and teaches me *lots* of words. Sometimes she reads me books with facts, but mostly it's stories. Stories are my favourite. She puts her finger under the words, and I put my paw on her hand, and that makes her laugh. It's a *very* good feeling to learn words: it's like eating magic and putting power in your brain. It makes me feel *very* happy in a way that feels endless, like looking into the night sky.'

'Oh,' says Malkin, 'that does sound wonderful.'

'Would you like me to teach you? I could try. We could start with the blackboard and then with the signs that sway, and the names of boats, and the things humans drop when they don't care.'

'I would like that very much.'

'Oh, I'm so glad. It *is* a special power, Malkin.'

'And counting?'

'Counting's easy! I can count to eighteen.'

'Eighteen? That sounds so many. I can only count to nine.'

'So I will teach you reading and counting. I'm sure it will help you. When the time comes … for you to leave.'

'Yes,' says Malkin, and his voice is sad, but then, in the second that follows, he sits upright, his ears back, his tail high.

'Oh, Malkin, what is it?'

But Malkin is silent, so Roux prods him with a paw.

'Oh, Roux! Something's wrong. I can hear someone crying. It's coming from down by the river; I have to go to help.'

'I'm coming too,' Roux says, getting ready to spring, but at that precise moment a pair of human hands lifts her clear off the ground. 'Go without me, Malkin,' Roux shouts down from the hands that are stroking. 'Run and see! I'll come as soon as I can. Careful, there's a human coming to pick you up too.'

So Malkin turns all his senses up sharply, crouches low, sticks his great tail in the air and takes an enormous leap in the direction of the river.

Chapter 7
The Swan

Down at the riverbank Malkin stops suddenly. He is filled with the most curious feeling. He can feel his sixth sense tugging him in one direction, and at the same time he can feel it tugging him in a different direction.

How can that be?

He knows he must move, but his sixth is confusing him, and the reeds are whispering in his ears, and behind is the noise of the pub, and somewhere nearby is the dull hum of cars, and sunlight is bouncing off the water, and the long grass is swaying, and a dragonfly is fixing him with its enormous eyes, and all the while there are the two tugs.

Malkin closes his eyes.

He knows instinctively what to do: he must turn off all his senses except for his sense of touch and his sixth. He sits still and wraps his tail tightly around his body.

Deep inside him, he listens to his sixth sense. Immediately it tells him there are two different places to go, so in his mind he marks the two paths and he leaps off to follow one of them.

'But I will help you too,' he says aloud, although no one can hear. 'I will come to you next, don't worry.'

Malkin's paws run over dry mud and damp mud. He runs blind, using his sixth sense and his whiskers to guide him along the river until he knows that he has found the place he needs to be.

Then Malkin turns all his senses up brightly and slows himself so that his movements are quiet and gentle. He treads softly until he reaches the voice that is crying. He can hear it clearly now.

'Oh, please can somebody help me? Oh dear, oh dear. Where are all my friends from our riverbank home?'

Malkin pushes his face through the tall bulrushes.

'Oh!' he exclaims, when he sees the white bird. 'Oh. You are like a queen.'

'A queen with no one to defend her throne! Oh, please will you help me? It's my eggs, my poor eggs.'

'Malkin sees she is sitting on a big, messy-looking nest on the riverbank.

'What are you?' Malkin asks.

'I am a swan.'

'Oh,' says Malkin. 'Swan.' He likes the word very much. It feels cool and peaceful, as if the word itself was born to float down a river. 'I've never seen anything like you. Your feathers glow white like the circle around my neck.'

'Oh, hurry, I am so afraid!' she says. 'He has eaten two of my eggs and now he wants to eat the rest!'

'Who wants to eat them?'

'He does.'

Just then a circle ripples in the middle of the river and through it appears a dark head, with small, bright eyes and sharp ears. 'Hungry,' the creature says, then disappears back under the water.

The swan rises in her nest and flaps her wings, flattening Malkin's fur with the great wind she creates. 'Oh no, oh no,' she cries. 'He's coming!'

'Eggs,' says the head, reappearing with another ripple, closer now. 'Hungry for eggs.' And it vanishes.

The swan stands in her nest. Malkin can see four eggs, big and white and shiny.

There is a gentle splash and the creature pulls its long sleek body out of the water. 'One egg,' it says. 'Gimme, gimme.'

Malkin speaks quickly. 'Sir, if you would like some food, I can bring you food.'

'What food, what food?' asks the creature, turning its bright little eyes on Malkin.

Malkin thinks about the blackboard. 'Lots of food. Any food you like.'

'Eggs I want,' says the creature. 'Eat them now I do, or I wait till your babies are born and eat them instead.'

The swan cries, 'Oh, I wish my husband were here.'

'Trapped he is,' says the creature, grinning. 'Downriver. Fishing line, caught his great big neck it has. Won't be seeing him again. Gimme egg.'

The swan hides her head beneath her wing.

'Please leave her alone,' says Malkin. 'I can get you food. Don't take her eggs.'

'Eat *you* I will,' says the creature, showing Malkin his sharp teeth. 'Eat you up, every bit.'

'Oh, please be careful,' wails the swan. 'He means it; he's very dangerous.'

'I don't like fighting,' says Malkin. 'I prefer peace.'

'Peace!' laughs the creature, and spits water on the riverbank. 'I hate peace, I do. *Love* fighting. I'm a *mink*. *Born* for fighting!'

And Malkin feels in his heart that this is true. The white hot flash of his sixth pulses through him and tells him he is in danger, terrible danger.

And now the mink is crouching low, his claws outstretched.

Malkin tries one final time, 'I can get you food if –'

But he gets no further than that, for that is the second the breath is knocked from him, there is the shock of pain through his neck, a screaming in his ear, and the world goes dark.

Chapter 8

Mink

Everything is sharp and sudden and furious. Malkin cannot see because his face is held down, pressing into the mud of the bank, but he can feel the claws and teeth that are tearing at him, sharper and more cruel than his own. He tries to turn and scratch, but this is a fierce enemy, and all the time there is the screaming sound of the mink's laughter, in his ears and in the air above him, and the distressed cries of the swan, and Malkin's sixth is going wild and he can't concentrate, can't think, not with all this sound and fury. And it is then he knows what to do.

He chooses that moment to turn off all his other senses and just use his sixth.

Everything becomes quiet. There is no sound and there is no pain. And in that space he can focus.

And immediately he knows three things.

The first thing is that he must fight or he will lose another life on this riverbank. He knows that the choice of peace has gone, for now.

The second is that he needs his tail.

Malkin's tail is squashed beneath him, trapped by the shock of the fall. If he can release it, then he will be able to spring and rise and push the mink from him, and then he will be able to fight.

The third thing is that he must trick the mink.

And Malkin knows at once what to do, and turns back on all his senses.

Malkin stops the struggle and lies flat and still, as if he has lost all his lives. The mink above him is triumphant, and lets out a shriek of glee. He takes his claws out of Malkin, stands on his hind legs and opens his sharp little mouth wide, ready to feast.

It is in that instant that Malkin releases his tail, lifts it high and rises up; and in the next those eighteen gleaming claws push free from the softness inside his paw pads and cut through the air with a wonderful sound that Malkin hears as he lands. Malkin feels his claws go through wet fur and into skin, and the warmth of blood that comes with the slice of claw that Malkin has never felt before, and does not like, and yet he knows that he has to do this to save his life and to save the lives that will be born from the swan's eggs.

The mink lets out a terrible scream of rage and pain.

The sound is so awful that Malkin lets go in an instant.

Malkin springs backwards on to the ground and stands surprised at what he has done. Then the mink lets out a low hiss and rises once more to its feet.

'And who's that?' it asks, looking behind Malkin.

'Watch out!' screams the swan.

And Malkin knows that something is wrong. Something is terribly wrong, because he can smell rain on grass and small flowers and all that is good in the world, and should not be in this place, not now.

'No!' he shouts, but the mink has already leaped over him.

Then the swan lets out a cry and Malkin hears a terrible sound. And Malkin fears he cannot turn, he cannot possibly turn, in case what he fears is true.

But he does turn.

And it is true.

Dangling in front of him is Roux.

She is held in the mink's sharp jaws and she is making little sounds of pain. Her paws hang limply from the creature's mouth and swing backwards and forwards against the fur on his chest.

Malkin cannot move.

He can do nothing.

He is paralysed.

He feels absolute and utter fear.

Which is when there is an almighty squawk and a swoop from the air, and Horatio is there, his claws knocking the mink down, and, in that moment of surprise, Roux falls limply from the mink's jaws and rolls away. Horatio lands. He stands above Roux, his legs a stockade around the injured cat. 'Fight, Malkin. I have her. Her best chance is if you fight. I will guard her. Quickly, he's coming for you again.'

And with that Malkin turns in the air, using his tail to rise, and with a sound that hurts the ears of all the animals, he lands on the mink with his claws out and his teeth biting into the soft fur beneath its throat. He bites in, and the mink shrieks and tries to wriggle free, but Malkin holds firm, then gives a great shake and the mink flies through the air and lands with a splash in the middle of the river, where it is swallowed immediately by the water.

The swan hisses and rises to her feet, but the mink does not reappear.

Malkin runs to Roux. Horatio steps aside.

And then Malkin lets out a terrible sound because the very worst thing is happening.

Roux is losing a life.

Chapter 9

Second Life

'Roux?' Malkin is saying into the darkness, and Roux can hear him, but his voice is very far away, her paws can't reach him and her eyes are too heavy to open. 'Roux, I'm here. It's going to be all right, I promise. Just let go. Let go of it, and the new one will come, and it will be beautiful.'

Roux can hear him, but it hurts where she is, all her senses hurt, and she is not sure if she *can* let go, because if she lets go, what then? Is it like falling from a very high wall?

'Paw promise,' she hears him say. 'I am here to catch you.'

It's Malkin, she thinks, deep in the place where she doesn't know what's real. This is Malkin and he is my friend. My very best friend.

So Roux lets go.

Inside her there is a *whoosh* of the brightest, lightest colours, and all the good feelings – from her first stroke by her Owner, to meeting Malkin, to the firefly of friend-ship, to exploring, to running along by the sea, to all the very best tastes and smells – all of it floods through her at once.

The strange feeling begins to pass. The lightness of sickening dreams ebbs away and the heavy, heavy tug of gravity is there. And Roux feels real again.

She opens pale green eyes, and finds sharp green eyes looking down at her, and black paws holding her through the feeling of falling that comes between lives.

'Oh, Roux,' Malkin says, 'I've been so worried.'

'Malkin!' says Roux. 'I thought … I don't know what I thought. I was in that creature's jaws.'

'Don't say it, Roux. I can't think about it. Does your neck hurt?'

'It does a bit,' she says, ruffling her fur. 'Urrgh, I can still feel those teeth in me. He bit into me, Malkin, he …'

'Shhh, Roux.' He buries his face in her fur and she feels that he is shaking softly from ear to paw. 'I thought I'd lost you. If it wasn't for Horatio …' Malkin looks up at the seagull. 'Thank you. I will be grateful till the end of my lives.'

'Don't mention it, chaps. Least I could do. Nasty creature that mink, killed a cousin of mine.'

'Malkin, your beautiful white circle, bits of it are gone and ... oh no, you're *bleeding*.'

'Oh, it's not serious. I didn't even lose a life, but you did and I feel so ...'

But Roux has put her paws around him and has buried her face in his neck, and Malkin finds that the feeling of her heart beating against his is the best feeling in the world.

After a few moments Horatio coughs softly. 'Excuse me, chaps, but if you'll not be needing me, I'll be heading off.'

And then Malkin remembers, and his sixth sense tugs in him again.

'Horatio, you have done so much, but there is still ...'

'Name it, Malkin.'

'We need your wings.'

'They are yours.'

'The swan has lost her husband. He's somewhere downstream caught in a fishing line. My sixth tells me he is still alive, but please will you go and look?'

'Of course.' And the seagull takes to the skies.

'Can you sit up?' Malkin asks Roux.

'Yes, I think so,' she says, and gets to her feet.

'We need to get you back to your Owner. You have a cut on your neck.'

'Yes, I need the stuff that stings and so do you, but if my Owner sees me she'll take me to the vet and I *hate* going to the vet. I *know* the vet is there to make us better, but somehow I always think she is going to make me worse. And I want to help, Malkin. Now, tell me, who were you helping? Was it that beautiful swan over there?'

'You're so clever, Roux. I didn't even know she was a swan.'

'I have watched her sailing along the river many times, but I've not seen her for a while. I can see it's because she's been sitting on her nest. Will you introduce me?'

'Of course.'

'Swan, this is my friend Roux. And my name is Malkin Moonlight.'

'I don't know how to thank you,' says the swan to Malkin. 'I don't know what words to say.'

'Oh, don't worry, swan,' Roux says. 'Malkin is the kindest animal in the world. He can't bear to see others suffering; he just *has* to help them.'

For a moment Malkin's fur feels hot and he looks at his paws.

'And the mink hurt you badly,' says the swan to Roux, 'and I couldn't help you, because soon my cygnets will hatch. I can feel they are almost ready and I cannot leave my nest because my husband is missing …'

Just then Horatio lands with a squawk. 'I've found him, but hurry, Malkin. He's caught in fishing line like you said and he's starving. Even if we manage to free him, he may not make it back to the nest. He's very weak: he needs food, and quickly.'

The swan lets out a great cry of pain.

'Sorry, ma'am,' Horatio says to her, bowing his head.

'Oh, swan!' Roux cries. 'What do you eat? What can I take him?'

'Water plants and small fishy creatures that you won't be able to find, but lettuce and bread will do,' says the swan. 'Oh, but please hurry. My poor husband!'

'Lettuce is easy, Malkin. The humans always leave the lettuce on their plates. Bread too.'

'You can't go on your own, Roux. You're not well enough. Horatio, will you fly with her? I can use my sixth to find the swan, and you can guide Roux back to the right place.'

'Right you are, Malkin. He's not far, not far at all.'

'Oh, I like my second life very much,' Roux says. 'It is full of excitement. I'll get the food, you free the swan – you know I'm an *extremely* fast runner, Malkin. See you soon.'

And with a whisk of her tail Roux runs through the start of her second life, while Horatio takes to the air and Malkin speeds off down the river, following the other path he has marked in his mind, as fast as his paws will take him.

Chapter 10
Lettuce and Bread

It hurts Malkin very much to see an animal so hungry and so unwell. But he has to put his feelings aside and concentrate on helping. The fishing line has caught the swan around his neck, and tangled around it in a tight ring. Malkin sees it will be very difficult to free him, because pulling one side of the line will pull the other even tighter. Malkin can also see that the swan has tried and tried to free itself. Now he is too weak to speak and his neck hangs limply.

He tries feebly to jerk away from Malkin.

'Don't move, oh swan,' says Malkin. 'You will make it worse. I am a friend of your wife, who is sitting on her eggs a little way along the river.'

The swan lifts his dull eye to meet Malkin's bright ones.

'I helped her against the mink and now I will help you.'

At the word mink the swan tries to flap his wings, but he is too weak to raise them very high.

'Please keep still,' says Malkin. 'I will be back.'

Malkin follows the fishing line along to where the other end is caught. He sees straight away what has happened. A careless fisherman has thrown his old line on to the riverbank and one end has become wound around a wooden post on the other side of the river and the other end around the poor swan when he flew into it. He has also left a plastic bottle on the bank and some other litter scattered about.

Malkin walks further along the river until he finds the narrowest crossing point. Although the river holds bad memories for him, Malkin is brave. He holds his great tail high in the air and takes a magnificent leap … and lands on the opposite bank.

Carefully, using his sharp claws, Malkin slices through the end of the line that is around the post. Then at least the swan is no longer tethered to the post and can move.

Next he leaps back over and returns to the swan. Saying reassuring words to him, Malkin nibbles through the line around the swan's soft neck. He is afraid that he is pulling, and that it must hurt, and for one terrible moment the swan jerks in pain, but finally he is free.

Straight away the swan puts his beak in the water to drink. He raises his head, breathes, then drinks some more.

After two long, cool drinks he lifts his dripping beak and asks, 'My wife?'

'Your wife is well.'

'And the eggs?'

'There are still four.'

The swan makes a low sound.

Just then there is a squawk and bread and lettuce fall into the water. The swan dips his neck and eats.

'Thank you,' says the swan. 'I fear I am too weak to sail up the river, but I need to see my wife.'

'Rest here a little,' Malkin says. 'More food is coming. Get your strength.'

'The mink,' the swan asks, 'did it eat our other two eggs?'

'I'm afraid it did.'

'But it has not harmed my wife?'

'It has not.'

'And those marks on your fur? Was that the work of the mink?'

And Malkin looks at his reflection in the water and sees that his white ruff is all pulled out in places, and Roux is right, he is bleeding. 'Yes, but it will grow back.'

Roux arrives on the bank, her mouth full of more bread and lettuce. She drops it into the water and the swan eats it hungrily.

'Oh, poor swan,' says Roux, seeing how thin and weak looking he is. 'I will run for more. Don't worry – I am very fast.'

'This is my friend Roux,' says Malkin, and looks away from Roux because she used to hum with the vibrancy of nine lives, and now she only has eight.

'Stop it, Malkin. I'm fine now, and I like this life. I couldn't stay a kitten forever. I can't spend all my lives in my basket and do no exploring or helping. That would not be living life at all well. Now, I will fetch extra bread and lettuce. I won't be long.' And she reaches out her nose and touches Malkin's nose, and for a moment they hold each other's eyes, before she turns and runs along the riverbank.

'The mink hurt your friend?' asks the swan softly.

Malkin shivers. 'It did. It took one of her nine lives.'

'I am very sorry to hear it. That mink came to our riverbank home a month ago. It has eaten the kingfisher and … done many terrible things. It wants to eat everything. It only thinks about killing. I hope it is gone for good. If you have got rid of the mink, you are a very brave cat indeed who has restored peace to our river community, and that is wonderful news for all the animals here.'

Just then more bread and lettuce lands in the water, with a squawk from overhead, and the swan dips and eats it.

'I am ready now,' says the swan, raising his long neck high, and Malkin sees that there is light in the eye that is regarding him. 'Thank you for your help. I will never, ever forget what you have done for me and my wife. I hope I see you again, if this is not to be my final journey.'

'I hope so too,' says Malkin. 'Goodbye, oh swan. Fare well.'

And Malkin watches the swan sail off slowly up the river.

'Come on, old chap, cheer up,' says Horatio, landing. 'Roux is with her Owner. She's being taken to the vet. She wanted me to tell you she's fine and she will see you this evening.'

'Oh,' says Malkin.

'Don't be sad, Malkin. The vet's the thing. They make animals better.'

'I know they do, but I feel very bad. I have helped others, but I have hurt my friend.'

'No,' says Horatio, 'that is not true. The bad mink hurt Roux, not you.'

'Roux has lost a life.'

'I know, but she still has eight, and that is a lot of lives to live. She told me that her second life is her favourite so far because it started with helping somebody. Go home and wait for her, old boy. You'll see her soon enough.'

But that night Roux is not allowed out. The window is kept shut all the way down with no air going in or out, and Roux is tucked firmly into her basket. She does not have a story time because she is already asleep.

Malkin sits all night on the window sill. He does not go into the cellar at all, but keeps his cold nose pressed firmly against the glass until the Owner gets out of her bed in the morning and he sees Roux leap happily out of her basket. Only then, on tired feet and with an aching neck, does he go down to the cellar, where he sleeps through the whole day, despite Roux putting the stuff that stings on him and wrapping him in her warm paws.

Chapter 11
The Vole

For a while Roux is looked after very strictly by her Owner and at night the window is kept shut, even though it is hot. Malkin's heart becomes heavy. He cannot tell the whole truth to Roux: that the pull to leave is getting stronger every day. Sometimes the tug is so strong that he feels sick, as if the sea is lifting him up and down, up and down, on the crossest of waves.

One night Malkin lifts his nose to the moon to ask for her help, but she has dark clouds dancing across her face.

Then, quite suddenly, he feels the call to help someone.

Immediately it makes him feel right and whole, and perfectly himself, as if this is who he was born to be.

It is coming from the riverbank, where he has not been since the day they helped the swans. Since that day Malkin has spent his nights cleaning litter away from the sea. There are so many things that are thrown in the water that hurt creatures big and little.

And there is another reason he has not returned to the riverbank: Malkin is afraid to because he is worried about the male swan.

He is worried that that swan did not manage to survive.

But now the pull is to the riverbank, and so it is to the riverbank that Malkin runs. He turns up all his senses brightly and in a moment he is down in the reedbeds and running like the very wind that combs his fur and whispers stories of its travels into his ears.

When Malkin sees the plastic bottle he is sad and angry. There is a very small creature trapped inside it. The creature is shaking so hard that Malkin fears for its heart.

'Please don't eat me, cat,' the creature cries in its pin-sharp voice. 'Please not.'

'I will not,' Malkin says. 'I promise. Don't be afraid. I'm going to help you. Stay at the bottom of the bottle while I slice the narrow end. Don't move – my claws are very sharp.'

The creature does not reply, so Malkin lifts his paw high and his claws come out with a slicing sound. He pierces the bottle and cuts the end clean away in one fell swoop.

I am stronger, Malkin thinks to himself, *and my claws even sharper.*

The creature rolls tightly into a ball at the end of the bottle, his tail wrapped around himself.

'Crawl out,' says Malkin. 'You must be hungry and thirsty. Come and lick the dew from the leaves and breathe the good air of the night. The worms are stirring under the earth and the grass is sweet.'

'No,' says the creature, 'I will stay curled up here. I will keep my eyes closed. So when you hurt me I don't see it.'

'What are you, creature?'

'I am a vole.'

'You are like a tiny mouse.'

'Not a mouse,' the little voice says. 'Vole.' And he peeps up at Malkin with shiny black eyes and sniffs the air with his little round snout. 'Ah,' he breathes. Then he shudders. 'Got in. Couldn't get out.'

'You are free now, vole.' Malkin walks a little way away from the bottle. 'I will not harm you.'

'Oh, the world smells good,' the vole says, and, with a little leap he lands in the reedbeds, where he drinks the dew. Then he burrows into the earth and hungrily eats the roots of the grass. 'I love life,' he says, munching.

When he is done he takes a final look up at Malkin.

'You're not like any cat I've ever heard of or seen. Thank you.'

He glances quickly from left to right, and Malkin watches him turn and scamper out of sight, into the safety of the long grass.

Which is when the moon draws a cloud from her face.

'It is right, Malkin Moonlight,' says the moon, appearing, 'to look after my rivers and seas. It is right to look after the creatures that live in, on and around them.'

'Thank you, oh Moon,' Malkin says, dropping a bow and pushing his nose into the grass.

'But what has happened to the ring I gave you?'

'It was a mink, oh Moon. He pulled the fur from me.'

'Then close your eyes, Malkin.'

And Malkin does, and at once he feels the wonderful racing along the paths of his blood and his sinews, and curling softly through his ears and tail, and tingling all along his whiskers, and finally ending deep inside his heart.

'Rise up, Malkin Moonlight.'

And Malkin does.

'Soon you will leave this place.'

'I know, oh Moon, for I feel the pull.'

'Yet you are sad. Do not be afraid of the pull. The pull is your destiny, and to be afraid of destiny is to be afraid of yourself. Remember all that is special inside you, all the good lives you are to lead.'

'Yes, oh Moon. I will.'

'But you know you have not yet found your home.'

'Oh, but I wish my home could be the cellar. I want to stay with Roux. I want to stay with her for …' But he finds he cannot finish.

The stars tinkle and tingle.

'Stars!' says the moon, and they fall back into the hum of their music. 'One day you will be called away to a new home, Malkin. You know that you must go when you are called.'

'I will go,' Malkin says, but his heart beats fast and his head fills with a picture of Roux.

'So you will. It will be a place where your kindness to animals is needed most. Be lucky on your journey, Malkin Moonlight.'

'Thank you, Moon, and goodnight.'

'Night is always good for me, Malkin,' the moon says, rising to illuminate the river. 'Now look.'

And Malkin looks to the river and sees two white swans sailing down its silver path.

'Oh!' cries Malkin, for in the next second he sees four small brown cygnets sailing behind them, down the curve of the river, and his heart explodes and his senses shine and the stars in the sky sing an octave higher for him.

Malkin Moonlight leaps an enormous leap, then runs towards his friends, crying aloud with all the joy a cat cannot contain.

Chapter 12
For Sale

A moon passes, as moons do, and the cats grow a little over that month, as little cats do. One morning Roux lands in the cellar full of excitement.

'Malkin! Malkin! Wake up. Come up to the pub! The men in helmets are on the scaffolding. They're hammering up a sign. Come on, you can read it, I *know* you can. You've been doing *so* well.'

The cats jump through the trapdoor and sit looking up at the scaffolding.

'Now look there, what does that sign say, Malkin?'

'I don't … It's hard … I don't know.'

'Take your time. Break it down. What are the capital letters?'

'There's an *F* for fish and an *S* for swan. I love the letter *S* – it's like a tiny drawing of a swan sailing that way down the river.'

'Very good, Malkin. Now, what about the small letters?'

'There's *or*, for if you'd rather do something else, and *ale*, for what the humans outside the pub drink.'

'Very good! Now put them all together like friends.'

'*F-or S-ale*. For Sale!'

'Well done, Malkin! It's a sign for the humans. It means that they sell a lot of things here: you can buy *tartine aux sardines* or *fromage*, or *steak frites* – *frites* means chips – like the ones you knocked over the other evening when you were running on the benches and the human with no hair shouted.'

'The chef had to come out and give him some more.'

'He was quite cross, but not as cross as that time when you smashed a glass with that great big tail of yours.'

'It was wrong of the human to trap the wasp like that. It was frightened.'

'The chef was *very* cross about the broken glass. He's always been kind to you, Malkin, and put out extra food.'

'I know, and I'm grateful. But it's not right for a creature to be trapped. Don't be cross, Roux.' And Malkin bumps his nose against hers, and bumps her with his head, until she laughs. 'You feel the same way: you gave one of your lives and now there are four new ones sailing down the river.'

74

For Sale

'Which reminds me, my Owner says I'm allowed out tonight.'

'Hooray! At last.'

'It's because it's a very magical night. I've just had a story about it. It's called Midsummer Night because it's the middle of summer: it's the longest day and the shortest night. There were beautiful pictures of flowers and fairies. Fairies are like tiny humans, but with wings and magical power.'

'I've never seen one.'

'I *think* I saw one once, but it might have been a butterfly: it flew *very* quickly. Perhaps we will see one tonight. Perhaps she will land in my red geraniums.'

'I hope so! How exciting. Imagine being able to fly, Roux.'

'Oh, I *wish* I could. It's strange though, isn't it, Malkin?'

'What is?'

'Why we need a new special sign high up when the blackboard already says what's for sale and there are other boards inside the pub, that tell the humans *perfectly* well what they can buy to eat. Why another sign? What do you think? What else could be for sale, Malkin?'

'I'm not sure, Roux. I can't think of a single thing.'

Chapter 13

Midsummer Night

Night takes especially long to come. In the end Malkin is so excited he arrives at the window box early and pushes his nose against the glass of Roux's window. A little sound escapes him when he sees Roux curled up in her basket, at the foot of her Owner's bed, looking very much as if she belongs indoors with her Owner and not outside with him at all.

Then pale green eyes, lit by the darkening light, appear on the other side of the glass. Malkin can't help it: he places his paw against the glass, and Roux places her paw against where his is. For a moment they look at each other, then Roux takes her paw away and noses out through the window.

'Did you see how long it took to get to night, Malkin? I've been so excited. Whenever I'm excited, things seem to take longer. What did you have for supper?'

'What you left out for me.'

'Is that all? You're growing so big. Look how you hardly fit into my window box now. Yet you are quite thin – you need to eat more than what I leave out for you. Perhaps you should kill a mouse.'

'Oh no, Roux! Never say such a thing. Mice are my friends; I share my food with them.'

'Oh, Malkin!'

'Please, you mustn't worry about me. I have everything I need.'

'Everything?'

'As long as I have you,' he says quickly and without thought.

Roux blinks at him.

Malkin feels his face grow hot and he gets a dizzy feeling, as if too many of his senses are busy at once. 'Let's climb on to the roof, Roux, and look out for magic.'

Roux looks up. 'But it's awfully high.'

'You'll love it, Roux, up high belongs to the moon and cats.'

'I'm not sure I'm brave enough.'

'Of course you are! Remember how you were afraid to jump over the seawall and then you loved exploring? Remember how brave you were at the riverbank? Please?'

'Oh, Malkin –' Roux smiles – 'I can never say no to you.'

The cats take a little leap, then climb up, up to the roof of the pub. The roof is not flat, but instead rises and falls in two sharp ear shapes, so they have to paw up one side, then slide down the other.

'Again!' says Roux, and so they paw up and slide, and paw up and slide, up and down the roof.

'I've never been so close to the moon!' Roux says, laughing.

'I knew you'd like it up high, Roux.'

Then they sit upon the big old chimney stack, squashed up, and for some reason the tips of their tails touch, then hesitate, then curl around each other like question marks.

Malkin turns to the crescent moon and tries hard to hear her, but she is too small tonight, just a cat claw in the sky.

'There's a blue moon next month,' Roux says. 'Two full moons in one month. I think special things will happen.'

'More special things?' asks Malkin.

'More.'

'I can't imagine anything more special than tonight,' Malkin says, looking at Roux for longer than he needs.

'Oh!' says Roux.

Malkin coughs. 'Roux,' he says finally, and doesn't manage more than that because suddenly all the things he has saved up inside – all the smells and flavours and sights and sounds and feelings – everything he has put a paw to, or his nose; every time he's used his tail to spring or to rise or fall, the friends he has made and the sounds he has heard and even the fight with the mink; all of those feelings are tumbling around inside him now. It is like being bright and light and without gravity all at once. Malkin thinks it must be how the fairies feel when they fly through the most magical of nights.

'Yes, Malkin?'

'I think I can feel magic. I think I can feel it all around.'

'Yes,' Roux whispers. 'I can feel it too.'

Malkin lifts his nose to her nose, and touches it against his; but it is not like the nose bumps of their infancy. It is something new.

Sharp green stares into pale green for a very long time.

And when they move apart they know that things are different.

Chapter 14
Lost

Everywhere Malkin goes for the rest of that moon, and into the next, he finds he thinks about two things:

The first is Roux. He thinks about her often and all the time. Even when he is thinking about something else, his thoughts go back to her without asking.

The second thought is about home.

The moon has said he is to find a new home, so Malkin knows his destiny does not end here. That the hour will come when the pull to his new home will tug at him like a big fat rope he saw on an anchored boat called *Fiesta*, bobbing against the tide. Then he will have to go, because he promised the moon, but he also knows he cannot leave without Roux. He can't leave her behind, because then whatever he finds will mean nothing.

He knows Roux thinks about it too. He can tell when she is, because she looks sad, and then she raises her eyes up to the room where her Owner sleeps. She can tell what Malkin is feeling and she knows that he can't stay here forever. But how can she leave?

Malkin wants everything to stay the same – but he can feel it changing all around, and he knows that change is right. He cannot stand on his back two paws and hold the leaves on the trees or the petals on the flowers when they want to blow away. He cannot persuade the moon to always be full, nor the birds to stay here. He can't tell the fish not to swim away in their underwater clouds. Yet all these changes feel like a threat.

There is only one thing he can do, but he does not know if it is what Roux would want. If she would agree to what he needs to ask her.

It is this that Malkin is thinking about when Horatio lands with a squawk.

'Ahoy there, Malkin. You look lost.'

'Can you be lost if you don't have a home?'

'Not as long as you have the sea and the sky.'

'Good,' says Malkin, 'then I'm not lost.'

The seagull turns his face sideways and his eye inspects the cat. 'Surely this is your home now, here with Roux. Do you plan to leave her behind?'

'Oh no, no. I could never do that. She is everything to

me. She is heaven and earth, Horatio, and more besides. More than I can dream of. Never. I could never leave her.'

It feels strange to Malkin to hear his feelings out loud, outside of himself. They seem to contain more truth, now he has told someone else, and that makes him feel happy and sad at the same time.

'So why do you want to leave, old chap? You have a friend and you have all the delicious fish a cat can eat.'

'There's something inside me – it's growing bigger and bigger, getting ready to pull me away.'

'I get the same pull in the evening, when all the seagulls take to the skies. It is a strong pull. I cannot resist it, I have to fly. I've seen starlings with it too – moving in great patterns. And the swifts and swallows get it very strongly – they have to fly all the way to Africa. Such a long journey. Where are you being called to, Malkin?'

'I'm not sure, Horatio. But I can't help feeling I have done and learned almost everything I can here. That there is more elsewhere. Somewhere I am needed.'

'And you need to know if your Roux will come with you.'

'That's it exactly, Horatio. But she is a Domestic. With a home and an Owner. And I am Wild, with nothing to offer her. Why would she leave her home for me?'

Horatio turns his head again and eyes the black cat.

'Because you are special, Malkin. Every creature around here knows it; everywhere I go I meet animals that you have saved or been kind to.' And he lifts his wing wide to show how far. 'Roux is not a kitten any more and, remember, there is a place I know of. A place that you and Roux could call home, if you wanted to. If you needed a place to go.'

'I do remember, Horatio, but you said it had some troubles.'

'That it does. That it does. But you could be the one to help, Malkin. Just say the word, old chap, and I will guide you there. The world is a beautiful place, whether you have paws or wings. But now is the time I must take to the skies. Think about it, my friend.'

'Thank you, Horatio. I just don't know why Roux would ever leave her Owner for me.'

'There is one reason, Malkin, and it is for her to decide, and her alone. I must away, my friend.'

And with that the bird salutes with one wing, and in the next moment, with a flap and a squawk, he is airborne.

Chapter 15

SOLD

It is a Sunday, the day that Malkin makes his decision. Tonight will be the blue moon, the magical moon. It is time to ask the Question. He looks sideways at Roux, sitting in the window box, and he sees how much she has changed.

The zigzags from her eyes are stronger and deeper, like they really intend to stay, and the fluff beneath her chin has gone and is smooth white fur. Her nine lives no longer hum from her, instead there are eight, but her exploring has given her maturity and wisdom. Malkin sees that she thinks a great deal more, and is no longer so ready to jump and pounce, but prefers to watch things and consider things and walk away from things with her tail held high, if need be.

'Malkin?'

'Yes?'

'I feel the oddest thing. Something inside keeps pulling at me. It keeps telling me I am to leave. Is it because you have to? And I should be with you? Oh, look, Malkin – the men in helmets are coming up the scaffolding with a new sign.'

'Oh, let me read it. S is so easy now – it is for our friends the swans. O is like the full moon. L is the corners where the mice hide. D is for dog – sorry, Roux. S-O-L-D: SOLD.'

'But what is sold, Malkin?'

Malkin considers this for a second. 'It must be all the food. It must have gone.'

Both cats look at each other and feel rather hungry.

'I have heard the chef say there is not enough fish left in the sea, but it can't *all* be gone. The sea can't be empty.'

'It cannot,' says Malkin. 'It cannot be empty, for the sea is the biggest thing there is, save for the sky.'

And suddenly Malkin feels an urgency inside him: a feeling of sparkles on water and sunrises that turn the sky into different shades and moods. 'Tonight, Roux, will you meet me on the seawall? It is the night of the blue moon. I want to ask you a question.'

Roux studies Malkin's face. 'Of course I will. But what

is it that you have to ask by the light of the blue moon? It must be very serious.'

'Meet me at midnight,' is all Malkin will say, but the way he says it gives Roux a feeling of sparkles and sunrises too.

Chapter 16
Blue Moon

When midnight comes the two cats sit on the seawall and look at the moon. She hangs low in the sky, keeping herself just above the inky black swallow of the sea's waves. The sea reflects the moon's image: round and full and doubly beautiful.

Malkin coughs a little cough, then takes a deep breath. 'Roux, to be with me means that one day you will have to leave your Owner.'

Roux pauses. 'I know that, Malkin. I have thought about it. I know I will be *so* sad to leave my Owner, but it would be so much worse to lose you, and it is your *destiny* to leave here, Malkin. We both know it. You have something special to do.'

'And will you come with me?'

'I will. Without you, Malkin, I would feel empty – like the sea if she lost all the things that live inside her. Or the moon on the nights when she is not there and is called new. I don't want to be new. I've *been* new, and you weren't there: there was my Owner, and good food, and books with pictures, and early bedtimes and that was enough for me. But I'm *not* a kitten any more, I'm a cat now, and I think about different things. The world is more than chasing my mouse and running fast. The world is all the things we can discover together.'

'You are right of course, Roux, because you always are.'

Then they turn, and Malkin looks into Roux's eyes. The moon floats behind them, creating their silhouettes against her vast white circle.

'So …' Malkin pauses, and inside Roux everything whirls and twirls. It feels like all the exploring they've done, all at once: like their first time over the seawall and their first run in the sand and … and scary, like the time she was held in the mink's jaws … and something else too, the same thing that she felt on Midsummer's Night on the rooftop, the thing that she first felt all those moons ago when she read Malkin's sixth. Something magical, deep and powerful.

Then Malkin takes a breath and he finds his words. 'Will you marry me, Roux?'

And Roux finds she needs no time at all.

'I will, Malkin.'

Malkin smiles, and both cats lift up their eyes and raise their heads to the night's starry sky.

'Please unite us, oh Moon,' Malkin says.

The moon beams down upon them. 'I see that you have followed your heart, Malkin, and you have found love.'

'I have, oh Moon.'

'And you, Roux?'

'Oh yes, Moon. I have.'

'Then I will unite you. Put your paws against your hearts and kneel down.'

The cats do.

'I unite you, Malkin Moonlight and Roux, as husband and wife, and I bless you. May your kittens' eyes ever be bright and their spirits pure, good deeds to do for cat-kind and for all. Let not time nor tide divide you. Now, Malkin, take Roux's left paw in your left paw, and you must both close your eyes.'

And, as the moon moves directly over them, the cats feel her power racing along the paths of their blood and their sinews, and curling softly through their ears and tails, and tingling all along their whiskers, and finally ending deep inside their hearts: small and precious and softly beating forever.

'Now rise up. Here is your gift. The circle and star I send are to remind you that you belong to one another and that you have my blessing.'

And at that a glowing star appears deep in the smoky fur of a toe on Roux's paw, which makes her gasp, and a pure white ring appears around the same toe on Malkin's paw.

Both cats are filled immediately and at once with the sensation of being given a new definition.

I am yours. You are mine.

We are joined as one.

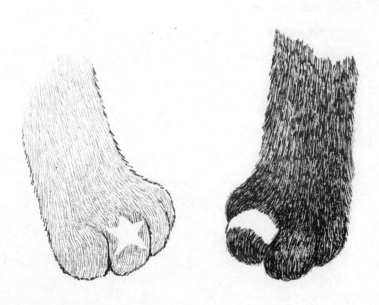

Then, in the second that follows, they feel the curiosity and wonder of being given a moon present.

'Thank you, oh Moon,' they say, their hearts beating with the blessing of the moon when she is at the height of her powers and the truth of their love that will never be divided.

'Go, and be together,' the moon says, rising to cover the cats in the luminescence of her light, while her stars begin to sing their sweetest songs.

Then Malkin and Roux rub into the soft fur around each other's necks and touch noses in a different way to all the times they've shared food. Malkin holds out a paw, and Roux takes it in hers, and the two cats dance under the magical light of a blue moon.

Chapter 17

Dog

In the morning Malkin wakes feeling wonderful. He checks the toe on his front paw.

And it is true. The little circle is glowing there. Roux is his forever.

He is so full of happiness he thinks he might explode.

Malkin jumps out of the trapdoor and into the blinking bright light of the morning.

Immediately his sixth sense burns.

There are three things wrong and they hit him all at once:

First – the blackboard has new writing. It says FULL ENGLISH.

Second – there is a strange smell.

Third – Roux is in danger. He knows it at once, as utterly and as completely as he knows himself.

In that second a sound escapes him, and the wind

grabs it and sends it travelling out to the deep blue sea. Malkin springs and runs past the benches and the black-board and ...

... and then he stops.

Two people walk out of the pub. The man has paint-ings on his arms. The woman puts something in her mouth and sets it on fire.

Malkin stares hard.

Then, from inside the pub, comes a terrible sound.

Malkin feels his back zip into a zigzag and his claws shoot out just as something huge and black bounds towards him with a studded silver collar and a great tongue lolling and dripping and sharp teeth biting together and springing towards him and ...

'DOG!' shouts Malkin, making himself thin and low and running. 'DOG!' And he bolts into the pub.

Everything is about shouts and screams.

The man Dog Owner is shouting in his deep voice and the woman Dog Owner is screaming in her high voice and Malkin is calling, calling for Roux, and the dog is barking and biting and the man Dog Owner is trying to hold the dog back by its spiky collar and the dog is trying to tear itself away and into Malkin, and still Malkin is shouting for Roux.

'Where are you, Roux?' he calls, but there's no answer, so he leaps up high and knocks a ship that is trapped inside a bottle off a shelf, and then he jumps along a ledge full of very old dusty things.

The dog gets free and jumps up at Malkin's tail, jumping and barking himself into a frenzy. Malkin just manages to get his claws into an old flag and lifts himself and his tail out of the dog's reach when the flag starts to rip and Malkin starts to fall.

In mid-air he has a choice: he could use the flag to jettison himself across the room …

… or he could fight the dog.

Malkin lets go of the flag, extends all his claws, and lands with his front paws on the dog's face and his back paws stuck into the ripple of muscles in the dog's back. His back claws push into the dog, and for a moment his front are free. He lifts them, as the dog lashes around, trying to throw him, then brings them down as hard as he can into the dog's face.

There is a yelp of pain, and then there is confusion.

Which is when Malkin springs for the door, and leaps into the sunshine and up the scaffolding, calling, calling for Roux.

The next moment the dog is at the bottom of the

scaffolding, barking and biting, drool from his mouth hanging from his loose pink gums.

Malkin looks through the window into Roux's room, but she is not there and her basket and toys are gone.

Which is when he hears her voice.

'Malkin! Malkin!'

An electric current runs through him and propels him up and across the roof tiles and scrabbling down the front wall of the pub, dropping to the ground just as the chef gets into the front of a blue car and Roux's Owner gets into the back, holding a cage. Malkin springs on to the car as the doors close and it pulls off into the road. He slides down it to sit at the back window, where Roux raises a cream paw and holds it against the bars that separate her from the window.

Malkin places a black paw against the glass. He can see she is crying.

But then the car speeds up, and speeds up more, and Malkin's claws scratch and screech against glass and metal, but there is nothing for him to grip. His claws slip and he is thrown into a hedge. He picks himself up and springs round on all fours, but even before he lands, with a spinning head and a bruised paw, even then he knows that Roux is almost gone.

He stands back up and lifts himself on to two paws just as the car zooms to the end of the road, then turns out of sight.

Malkin lets out a howl.

Roux is gone.

Chapter 18
A New Home

Half a moon passes. The beach gets very busy. Children are everywhere. It is hot and Malkin has to find shade when the sun is strongest to keep his black fur cool. By night he sleeps in snatches under a stripy beach hut. The rest of the time he looks for Roux. He uses all six of his senses, and still he cannot find her.

Horatio lends his wings to the search, while Malkin is on paw. Each dusk Malkin returns to the seawall in case Roux comes home, and from there he notes the changes.

The smell of the food changes.

The scaffolding comes down and is taken away on a low loader and the men in helmets leave.

SOLD comes down.

The red geraniums start to wilt and look sad because the new humans do not put water on them, like Roux's Owner did.

The dog patrols around, growling, and Malkin shivers, despite the warmth of the evening.

Late one afternoon Malkin is walking, like he does every day. He walks and walks, and he looks and he smells the air and he uses his sixth and listens to his heart but still he cannot find her.

The sea has grown quiet, the sun is low in the sky and Malkin's paws are dragging in the sand when a sweet smell travels to him. The smell he loves best in the world.

But he does not believe it.

Yet the smell comes again.

No, he thinks.

His paws lift and he begins to run. He sees prints in the sand. Leading back and forth from his beach hut to the seawall.

He runs faster.

His sixth sense starts to light up and move through him, bright and white.

And then he slows down.

The shape of the cat sitting on the seawall is the same. But the sad slump of her is new.

Nevertheless it is her.

His paws fail him.

His body stops still but his scent travels.

Roux opens her eyes. 'Malkin?' she whispers, then, 'Malkin!' she cries, and with a bound she is off the wall and into the soft sand and in the next second they are together: paws together, ears together, necks wound round one another. Then they roll over and over, tumbling as they did as kittens when the world was playful and made for fun.

Then Malkin stops and moves away from her.

'There you are,' he says. 'At last it's you. I thought you'd forgotten me.'

'It would be easier to forget myself.'

He places his left paw on her heart. And she places her left paw on his.

'The chef opened a new restaurant on the other side of town. It's called La Chatte Grise. My Owner kept me inside one room and would not let me out for half a moon – it is a rule of moving. I tried and tried to escape. Today was my first chance so I took it. I had to be with you.'

'I'm so happy I have you back, Roux.'

There is a squawk, and Horatio lands. 'I've been flying everywhere for you, shipmates. This is perfect: you've found each other and I've found a way to your new home, if you want it. If you're coming you'd better make it now, and quick.'

'New home?' Roux asks.

'We can't go back to the pub, Roux: there's a dog. It's the day we knew would come.' Malkin puts his nose against her nose.

'Oh, Malkin,' says Roux, 'I've left my Owner. It's done. I want to be with you. Wherever that may be. Take off my collar.'

'Are you sure?'

'I am.'

So Malkin gently bites off Roux's collar and it falls to the sand. Roux shakes her neck and ruffles out her fur. 'Now, what is this place, Horatio?'

'It's a Recycling Centre, where the things humans don't want go to be made new. There are good cats there; it's a community. There are no Owners, but the cats look after each other. But I must warn you chaps, there is danger, there are troubles.'

'If there is danger and trouble then Malkin will help,' says Roux. 'I know he will. Where is it, Horatio?'

'It's a long way on little cat feet, but the good news is today is Rural Skip Day.'

'What What Day?'

'Men in gloves take skips to pick up things from places that are far from the city. Then they bring them to the

Recycling Centre to be sold in the Re-Use Shop. So you travel there by skip! It's a watertight plan, chaps. Be there in no time. Follow me. We must be quick – the men take away the skip at sunset.'

And the cats race off, full of life and love, following the shadow of Horatio dipping low and calling to them, 'You must get out of the low loader before you get to the centre. You don't want to be poured out or you'll be squashed. They'll hold it up high and tip it. It would be, frankly, chaps, a disaster. Jump out at the traffic lights – you'll see the sign. Now, come on, run like your hearts are in it.'

The men in gloves have just put the skip on the back of the low loader and are finishing their flask of tea. The two cats jump into the skip and settle among some wooden chairs.

'All aboard!' Horatio calls from the sky. 'Heads down. And we're off.'

The engine begins to rumble and the seagull looks at the two cats wrapped in each other's paws. 'Excuse me, folks. I'm flying ahead,' he squawks, 'I'll see you there. See if they've saved a bite to eat for my supper.'

The cats watch Horatio take to the sky as the low loader takes to the road, rumbles slowly down the High Street, then speeds up.

'Hold on tight, Roux!' says Malkin.

'This is *exciting*, Malkin. Oh, this feels like adventure.'

A short while later the engine stops and two heads pop out of the skip.

'This is it,' says Roux. 'Look – there's a big green sign that says "Starcross-on-Sea Recycling Centre". Let's jump out while the traffic light is red.'

The cats jump out and land on the pavement. They run towards the sign and make a leap together on to a stripy barrier marked 'Entrance/Exit'.

'This is our home, Roux. Our new home.'

As Malkin says the words, tall floodlights come on and bathe the centre in light.

'Oh,' says Roux. 'This place is enormous!'

'Ready to jump?'

'After five?'

'After five.'

Together they count to five, then jump down. As they walk Roux winds herself close to Malkin. She does not say that all of a sudden she misses the sea, and the smell of French food, and her Owner very much. She decides to be brave, to be very brave, for Malkin.

Then she jumps backwards. Her sixth sense feels hot, like touching her nose against her water bowl when it has been in the sun. She looks up at the long, high wall that runs all the way along the very edge of the Recycling Centre.

'Oh, Malkin, there's something strange. Something not quite right. Do you feel it? It must be the trouble that Horatio warned us about.'

Malkin does feel it. He feels it all around. He looks up at the wall. It makes his fur rise in waves and pulls at the claws inside his paws. Yet there is another feeling, a good feeling, that this is the place that has been calling him. The pull to move has stopped, the achy feeling inside him is all gone. He is sure they have found their new home. He is about to tell Roux all these good things when there is a crashing noise, which makes her jump in the air.

'It's just the men in gloves emptying the skip, like Horatio said they would. Shall we climb that wall? Get a high-up view?'

'Ahoy! Shipmates, you made it, you made it. Now come away from that wall, Malkin, it's this way.' Horatio swoops low and veers away to the right. 'Your new friends are waiting for you in Glass Bottles and Jars. That's it, chaps, follow me, follow the wind, it's blowing in the right direction. Hurry – the clouds have turned inky and soon the moon will rise. I must away, it's past my bedtime; I'll need a star to steer by.'

So for now the cats put away their thoughts and chase after the shadow of the seagull as he swoops under the floodlights and into the dark depths of the Recycling Centre.

Chapter 19

Friends

Malkin can feel five eyes watching him as he walks into Glass Bottles and Jars. He can't see the eyes, but he can feel his slim silhouette being reflected on five shining retinas. He looks to check Roux is just behind, then makes a magnificent leap, as if he's cut off his deal with gravity, and for a fraction of a second he's off all four paws, suspended in the air. Then he lands delicately with no sound on top of a large green bin.

His sixth sense shines from him, radiating in iridescent waves, like the colours on a moth's wing. Every fibre of his fur is upright, a crazy silhouette, prone and ready. His great tail sticks up into the sky behind him like a rocket hoping to find the moon.

'That is a rare cat and no mistake,' says the blue cat with orange eyes, who is called Marmelade.

'Oh, I say,' says Sonata, in her sing-song voice.

Foss's claws come out and slightly scrape the wooden wine crate that he's standing on. Sonata hears and turns to shine her two brilliant blue eyes on his one lonely amber one. The beauty of her white fur in the moonlight holds Foss's attention for a moment, and he blinks at the curve of the waxing crescent moon, a shimmering white claw, captured in each of her eyes. Her perfection stills Foss and then a mew escapes, and he has to turn his face from her and wrap his tiger-striped tail tightly around himself. His claws crack back into the crate as he thinks about the new cat.

'Stop that, Foss,' Sonata says, 'Horatio says this cat is going to be our friend. You must welcome him, not fight him.'

Foss makes his claws retract and sit inside his paws, but his orange body stays tense and prone.

'And, Foss, perhaps this cat could be the fighter that we need,' Sonata says. Then she pauses, and she almost doesn't say it, but she does, in the quietest voice she can, 'Since we lost Sage.'

And five eyes close as they watch their ghostly memories of their friend run through their minds and they feel the loss of him in their hearts and whiskers and the cold pads of their paws. Sage who was good, and wise, and kind.

'He will fight well, *chérie*,' says Marmelade. 'You are quite right – just look at how he uses that tail of his. It is a magnificent tail. He is a Wild one and no mistake, but he has great strength and beauty; I recognise this. It was the same with my ancestors. They were very strong, like him. They had to live Wild after their Owners had their heads chopped off during the revolution.'

Just then a cat the colour of smoke and cream lands too.

'Oh,' says Sonata. 'Look how soft her fur is.'

'Too soft,' says Foss, raising his stripy tail. 'Too much of it.'

'*Mon Dieu*,' says Marmelade, 'that cat's fur is *very* soft. That girl is a Domestic, you mark my paws and whiskers. There is something French about her: look at her nose – it dips, then goes up to the sky like mine. She will find it hard here at first: with the food from old cans and the outside sleeping. Very hard. Sonata, we must help her feel at home; we must help her understand this is a lovely home to have.'

'We will, Marmelade. We'll be her friends. We'll find her the finest food we can.'

'That is very good, *chérie*.' And Marmelade smiles a wide blue smile into the night and flashes her marmalade-coloured eyes. 'We will look for the caviar.'

Sonata starts as Dew appears, as Dew does, being a friend both of shadows and of coming from nowhere. He springs to the top of the bin and moves close to the black cat with the magnificent tail.

'Welcome,' he says.

Even though the little silver-grey cat is unthreatening, Malkin takes a step backwards, closer to Roux. He has never met a cat with only one life before. The feeling makes Malkin's head spin. One life. Malkin does not know how he will live when he has only one left, but he suspects he might stay inside a box, or under a beach hut, or on the highest wall and never come down. But as long as he has Roux it will not matter. And of course *she* will always have eight. She can never have fewer than eight. And Malkin knows Roux will make sure he is looked after and not alone when the final one goes.

Malkin feels sorrow flood through him like a rising tide. He looks at the cat with one life and considers his must be a very sad story, this poor cat.

Dew feels Malkin's concern and walks slowly along the edge of the bin, full of balance. He lifts his paws and stops light and exact in front of Malkin. Malkin sees that his eyes are the same colour as his fur. They are full of silver light.

'You mustn't worry about me, friend,' Dew says. 'My lives have all been glorious – each and every one. My eight have been well lived and I have nothing to regret. You can use your sixth to read me, if you would like.'

Malkin closes his eyes. Immediately, in his sixth sense, he sees the lives that Dew has lived and he is flooded with warm feelings of friendship and wisdom and kindness. There is some sadness, but Dew has wrapped it up with love and light, so that it does not hurt.

Malkin opens his eyes.

'My name is Dewey but my friends call me Dew, for short.'

'My name is Malkin Moonlight and this is Roux. The moon has united us in marriage and now we're looking for a home.'

Dew's bright eyes move east to west and back again in tiny rapid movements, as if he is reading the new cats. Then he smiles a soft smile that raises his whiskers. 'You're very welcome here, Malkin and Roux. Please jump down and meet the others.' He leaps to a cardboard box, then springs the rest of the way to the ground.

'Come on, Roux,' Malkin says quietly, feeling her fear. 'He's kind and good.'

'I know – it's just … it's just that other thing that I said before: there's something strange here. Something I feel afraid of. It must be the trouble that Horatio warned us about. Don't you feel it, Malkin?'

'I do feel it, Roux, but I'm not afraid. I think the feeling is there because this is the place where I am needed. It means I am in the right place. It is like the feeling I had just before we helped Horatio, and the time we were called to help the swans, and all the times I've been called to help the little and big creatures of the sea and river.

But it is stronger still than any of those, far stronger; there is danger here, like there was with the mink, but this time it is covered up in a good feeling.'

'I will try to be brave then, Malkin. If this is the place where you are needed.'

'Thank you, Roux.' And Malkin puts his paw on her paw, and his moon ring and her moon star glow in the night. 'Now let's go to meet the rest of our new friends. Are you ready?'

'Ready.'

So Roux and Malkin turn and jump to the ground, allowing gravity back into their lives.

Chapter 20
The Things People
Throw Away

Sonata leaps to sit with the new cats in Glass Bottles and Jars. Foss watches her purring softly and tries, and fails, to keep his claws inside. His voice mews out long, like a stretch of elastic. 'Tell us your story,' he says to Malkin and Roux. 'Why have you left your home?'

Malkin twitches back his ears, then moves them forward again and looks at Roux. Roux looks at her paws.

'You are Domestic, *chérie*?' Marmelade's voice is soft. She is sitting on an upside-down box that has blown over from Cardboard/Paper.

'I was. I had an Owner. A girl …'

'A girl!' say all the cats together. Ahhh, they breathe,

feeling the stroking feeling, feeling the purrs growing in the furnaces deep within them where purrs are made.

Roux nods. She is about to explain that her Owner's name is Cecilia and she is the chef's daughter and that it is very nice to hear Marmelade's French accent because it is like a tiny taste of home, like licking the chef's fingers when he fed her, but she holds all that in because she thinks her voice will break up like the sound of the skip being emptied and everything smashing as it hits the ground.

Dew speaks to Malkin, sensing Roux's sorrow. 'Did the girl love Roux? Was she a kind Owner?'

'Oh yes. She loved her very much and she was a very kind girl.'

The cats fall into a quietude.

Foss breaks it. 'So why did Roux leave her Owner? Don't tell me it was to follow you.'

Malkin coughs, and pulls himself as upright as a sitting-down cat can be, and raises his great tail behind him. 'It was. I am Wild. I was put into a bag with my sister and brothers and thrown into a river.'

'Oh dear,' says Sonata. 'The things humans throw away.'

'I washed up near Roux's pub and she saved me. Roux lived in the pub and I was allowed to live underneath in the cellar. The chef fed us French food. We spent the days exploring: running wild, chasing each other with the wind in our fur, fast as magic. We ran by the sea and we explored the riverside. We made friends and helped other animals. Roux became very brave: she even sacrificed a life to help a nesting swan. We grew big and strong. We kept growing: especially me. We had many happy moons.'

'A good life,' says Dew.

'It was,' said Malkin, 'but I have always felt there is more. When the moon named me, she said I had a destiny.

More and more I felt the need to leave. But I couldn't leave Roux. I wished that –'

'Wishing is a waste,' interrupts Foss.

'There is a lot of waste in the world,' says Sonata gently, 'but *wishing* is never wasted, Foss.'

Foss sticks his nose up at the stars.

'… I wished that Roux would come with me. So one night I asked her if she would marry me, and she agreed.'

'Ah!' says Sonata.

'This is a very beautiful story,' says Marmelade.

'The moon united us on the seawall when she was full. We were very, very happy.'

'You were united by the sea?' Dew asks. 'At night? Under a full moon?'

'Yes,' Roux answers in a small voice. 'In fact it was a *blue* moon. Why, Dew?'

'Well,' says Dew, 'it is very powerful when you are united by the sea. The love is very strong. It seems to stretch further.'

'Really?' asks Roux, feeling quite happy for a brief twitch.

'Oh yes, Roux,' says Dew, 'and at night: the night sky stretches to infinity. It is vast. To combine the sea and the night and the power of a blue moon – well: your love is very powerful.'

Roux feels a swelling of affection for this poor cat who only has one life.

'But what went wrong, *chérie*? Something must have gone terribly wrong for you to leave your Owner, and your pub with its French food. What is the truth of your story?'

The darkness thickens in a comforting way around the cats, and in the stillness of the Recycling Centre at night lies the dark blank space for the rest of the story.

Roux drops her chin, closes her eyes for a blink and her ears for a flick.

'Well, Marmelade, you are right: something went wrong. First the signs went up: "FOR SALE". And then one day the sign changed to "SOLD" and we thought it meant the fish but one morning my Owner put me in my cage and said not to worry. She took me down through the pub and told me that it had new Owners. Dog Owners.'

'*Mon Dieu!*' Marmelade puts a blue paw to her mouth.

'I saw the dog just before I was put in the car. A great big horrible dog. I cried for Malkin and he came running and jumped on the car, but it went so fast that he was

117

thrown off into a hedge and I was so frightened that he might have lost another life.'

'And I was so frightened that I would never see Roux again. The pull to leave that place got worse and worse, but I could not. I slept under a beach hut and kept looking and looking for Roux. Horatio looked from the skies, and I looked from the ground, and then, today, she was back again.'

'I'd been kept inside one room because we had a new home and I was not allowed out for half a moon. But, finally, today a window was left open, and I escaped, and I ran a long, long way to find Malkin, and I was very afraid because it was so dangerous; I had to cross roads and go all the way along the beach, but I found him, and then we threw my collar away, and Horatio told us about here, and now we have come looking for a new home.'

'Well, *chérie*, it is not perfect here, but this Recycling Centre is a good home. It is full of love and kindness and plenty of food and clean water. Also there is a whole section where the milk cartons go. And there is fish from the sushi restaurant in the city. It has its own industrial wheelie bin. It throws away so much you cannot believe it. Have you eaten sushi, Roux?'

'I haven't.'

'It is fish the chefs have put in circles, *chérie*. It is very delicious. So if you want to stay here, you have found your home. There is something that we have to tell you, if we are to be perfectly honest with our new friends, but it can wait until tomorrow. You must be tired. You have had a lot of excitement in this one day.'

'Yes,' Dew says, 'and I expect neither of you has eaten. Help yourselves to any food you find.'

'We sleep over in Mattresses,' says Sonata, who has jumped to the ground and is lengthening her pure white body and stretching her claws. 'It's in that direction,' she says, turning her head and pointing with her nose. 'Are you ready, Marmelade?'

'Born ready, *chérie*.'

The moon is high in the sky and the pull to hunt is becoming more insistent.

Sonata feels the shared need, the growing ache, to run and pounce. She knows that when she is hunting with Foss they will be united by basic, delicious primeval feelings, and the sadness about his eye will be forgotten for a while. They will become the same as their ancestors: the African wildcats who ruled the savannas and who were born to kill. When she looks at Foss she sees the wildcat in him, in his markings and in his face; he wears his

119

wildness close to the surface of his fur, and she finds it very beautiful, although she has never found a way to tell him that. Once she feels they were both so close to admitting their feelings, but then the terrible fight happened, and Foss lost his eye, and things changed between them.

Foss feels the sinews in his body are taut like violin strings. He stretches his front paws out, but still the need to spring is wound up vicious and small inside him. He looks for a second at Sonata, then quickly turns his head away. 'Ready, Dew?'

'Yes,' Dew says, rotating his ears and moving his whiskers up and down. 'Malkin and Roux, you are welcome to join the hunt, if you'd like to.'

Malkin looks at Roux. She is so tired that her whiskers are drooping. 'Not tonight, thank you. To be honest, we don't hunt. We've always been given food.'

'It's not for the food,' says Foss, beginning to head into the deeper darkness. 'We have plenty of food here. I am a working cat, like my parents before me and their parents. We don't want vermin running around like …' But Foss falls quiet, and Malkin thinks of the rats he has played with and the mice he has shared his food with and he too is silent.

120

Dew nods at the high wall that runs along the edge of the bins. 'Just don't go over the wall, whatever you do. We'll explain tomorrow.'

'We'll see you at dawn,' says Sonata as she slips into the black spaces between the bins with Marmelade. Dew follows swiftly behind, a darting silver-grey shadow, like the fish Malkin used to watch beneath the surface of the river by the reedbeds. His voice and his silhouette vanish into the darkness and the four cats are quite gone.

Just then a gust of wind comes careering around the corner. It blows a box up to where Malkin and Roux stand.

It lands with a clatter so unexpected that Malkin pounces backwards, tail erect, claws out. Then he sees it is a box, just a box, and he feels foolish for a second and then curious into the next. He smells a smell he knows so well, a smell he recognises in the deepest parts of him. He looks at Roux. She smells it too.

Even before Roux flips open the lid, the cats know what they are going to find and then there it is: half a *tartine aux sardines* inside a crumpled serviette.

Roux sits on her back paws and pulls the *tartine* in half, passing half to Malkin. It tastes the same as the chef's *tartine*, and it makes them both mew.

It is like eating memories.

For a while afterwards the cats sit still, with their eyes closed, remembering the day that Malkin was washed up. For Malkin it is strange to think that that day of all days – the day after the night that tried to kill him – was the happiest of his life, because it was the day that Roux found him.

Roux looks at Malkin. The food inside her is giving her strength, and she finds her determination humming back: the same determination that got her away from La Chatte Grise and a very long way across the town, all the way back to Malkin on the beach. 'Come on, Malkin,' she says, 'let's find Mattresses.'

So the cats set off, looking up at the signs until they read one that says 'Mattresses'. Then they turn down an alleyway and they are there.

Roux allows the tiredness to hit her, and her paws to lose their spring, and her tail to droop. Malkin watches her trail along, full of heaviness, with slump in her tail. Usually this time of night is when they feel most awake, most active, most alive, but tonight, all of a sudden, he too is dragged down by tiredness.

It is a vast area, with mattresses stacked high and scattered wide. The cats sniff their way through until they pick up the scent of Dew on one mattress, and Foss at the bottom of another, and Sonata who sleeps at the top of the one next to it, and Marmelade on another, very thick, very springy mattress.

Malkin picks a mattress that belongs to no cat. It is almost fresh. He claws a bit with his front paws to release the fluff inside, then claws a bit with his back paws. Roux helps him. It would be fun – like being kittens again – if they both weren't feeling so tired, but they find they have absolutely no energy, so they bury themselves inside the fluff until they are quite warm.

Then, for the first time in half a moon, Malkin's heart is light because he can feel Roux breathing next to him.

So he closes his eyes.

And that night, in their dreams, they run together by the sea.

Chapter 21
Stories

Malkin wakes up feeling wonderful. The mattress he is on is so soft and his dreams have been beautiful and have restored him.

'Breakfast, Malkin!' Roux is saying as she shakes him with her paw. 'I've been up for *ages*. We have to go to Glass Bottles and Jars again to meet the others. We're going to have breakfast and share stories. I feel *so* excited. I *do* like our new home. I've been talking with Marmelade. She's invited me to visit her in Small Domestic Items; apparently she has her own armoire. I didn't know cats could be blue – I know I can't see colour very well, but she tells me she is the most *exquisite* shade of blue. And Sonata has promised to teach me to sing. I can't help staring at her: she's as white as the moon. I can't work out which fascinates me more: blue or pure, pure white. Come on. Get up!'

Malkin gets up and both cats head over to Glass Bottles and Jars with a spring in their paws. Around them lorries come and go, beeping backwards and emptying their contents into the different bins in the different sections. A man wearing gloves stoops to stroke first Roux, then Malkin.

'New cats,' he says. 'Pretty ones. Keep the mice down for us.'

Malkin mews back, but the man doesn't understand him.

All the cats, save for Dew, are sitting around waiting to eat. There are six glass containers of food shared out on the ground and one quarter-full plastic bottle of milk. Dew is sitting on a low bin marked 'Jars', looking about nervously, his whiskers twitching.

'Oh, thank you very much,' say Roux and Malkin, seeing the food set out nicely.

'This one is yours, Roux,' says Sonata. 'We have found some special food for you. Marmelade says you will like it because it's French.'

'Oh, that *is* kind. Gosh, this is all so civilised, isn't it, Malkin?' Roux says.

'What's civilised?' asks Foss.

'It's sharing food and keeping your paws clean,' Sonata

says, 'and not going to do your business in the wide open. It's going behind boxes, or in the litter tray if you have an Owner.' Then she adds more softly, 'Not that you ever had an Owner, my darling, but you are still *very* civilised.'

Foss turns his face away. The *darling* has made his blood race hot and his face turn warm. Even his tiger stripes feel as if they are burning orange. He closes his eye and waits for the feeling to pass.

'I think it's more than that,' says Malkin, settling down to eat. 'It's being kind to everyone. It's showing kindness to creatures who have less than you, even the ones who are unkind to you.'

Sonata looks at Marmelade for a moment and then up at Dew.

There is something left unsaid. Malkin can feel it in the air around him like he can feel the electricity that runs through the pylons above them.

'Malkin *loves* helping others,' explains Roux, licking a paw. 'It makes him *very* happy because he is *exceptionally* brave, and when he can help another animal it fills his sixth sense with the best feeling. It is as if he has no choice some-times – he just has to be kind to others. He's a very special cat – that's why the moon gave him a present.' She turns her pale green eyes to look at Malkin, and he feels the warm flow of his love for her course through his veins and end up as a tingle in his whiskers.

Roux continues. 'I had a feeling that Malkin was being called here for a reason, but I can't see what it is. You're all so happy; you don't need any help. I do wonder what it could be. Although there *is* a strange feeling in the air, particularly if I look over in *that* direction.' And Roux indicates the great wall with her upturned nose.

'This is true, *chérie*,' Marmelade says. 'This is the thing I said we would tell you today, to be perfectly honest with our new friends. We have talked and it is decided: Dew will tell you after breakfast. It is best coming from him. He has the words. He has read a lot of books.'

'But first enjoy your breakfast,' Sonata says, 'and we will tell you our stories, because you told us yours last night. Then we will all know each other a little better and that is how friendship is made. Marmelade, you should start. I expect your story will be the longest.'

Malkin is interested to learn the other cats' stories, but his sixth sense is thrumming with the need to know what is on the other side of that wall, and why it is pulling so strongly at him, almost as if *that* is the side he should be on, not this.

'*Oui*, I will begin,' says Marmelade. 'I am a pure-blooded Chartreux, which is why I am this particular shade of blue.' She pauses to ruffle up her coat so it sits about her, double-thick. 'My great-great-grandmother, Confiture, lived in the Palace of Versailles.' She curls her blue tail around her waist like a belt. 'My Owner was descended from *noblesse d'épée*, before the commoners took away the family title during the revolution. Then her family had to move to England to escape the guillotine and they brought my ancestor with them. But that was all long ago. Last year my Owner died. When the house-removal men came I hid inside my Owner's armoire and was brought here. Now this is home. It is a very good home, but without my Owner I have one sadness – it is a great sadness.' She flashes her marmalade-coloured eyes at the cats. 'Only a human can see the *exact* colour of my beautiful eyes and the *precise* glorious shade of my fur: this is why my Owner named me Marmelade – on account of my eyes. You and I cannot see my true beauty, with our eyes that work so well at night but were not made for appreciating colour. It is the great tragedy of my life here.'

'I can *imagine* that your eyes are a very beautiful colour,' says Roux in a hushed voice.

'*Oui*. Precisely. You have to imagine. And now every Monday the men in gloves come and try to take away my armoire because a human has chosen it. It is the only thing I have left, the only vestige of the life I had when I had an Owner. So I have to defend it with tooth and claw.'

A gentle wind ripples through the centre, singing over glass and rustling plastic bags and paper, and on it is carried a peculiar smell that Malkin cannot identify.

Malkin turns to Foss. 'I see you've met unkindness, Foss. What happened to your eye?'

Which is the worst thing he could say.

Foss bristles. His claws shoot out. The wood beneath him groans and creaks its pain. Sonata purrs softly, 'He didn't know not to ask, Foss.'

Foss closes the embarrassment of his one eye and turns his face away from them all.

'He doesn't like to talk about it,' explains Sonata, moving across the crate, tilting her softness and the warm hum of herself towards Foss's tiger-striped fur, remembering the cat he'd been when he had two eyes. She stands close to him until she hopes his bad feelings have broken up and become mashed and compressed into something smaller.

'I'm sorry,' Malkin says. He puts his nose to the wind. The smell has come again.

'Now it is my time,' says Sonata in her gentle sing-song voice. 'I was a cathedral cat. I was employed to keep the mice out of the old astronomical clock. But what I loved best was helping the choristers with their singing and pressing the buttons on the organ and watching the humans ring the bells. I am very musical. I love music. It is sad for me that there is so little music here: just bottles with water in them, and the wind that sings, and the hum of the pylons, and sometimes a musical instrument in the Re-Use Shop: but the humans buy them quickly and the men in gloves tell me off for touching them. Particularly the guitars.'

'But what happened?' asks Roux. 'Why did you leave the cathedral?'

'The old dean died and a new dean came. He had his own cat, a big black cat named Rocket who was terribly aggressive. He said it was his cathedral now and he would get his Owner to get rid of me. He used to crouch under the pews and spring out to frighten me. He would climb up the bell ropes and jump down on me. He had very sharp claws. I became unhappy. I was thin and my fur started to fall out. I was jumpy everywhere I went.'

'So what did you do?' asks Malkin, feeling distressed for Sonata.

'The new dean had his house on Cathedral Green renovated. A skip was put outside and the old furniture put in. One day I felt the pull, a really strong pull, to get into the skip. So I did, and I ended up here, in the Re-Use Shop, and I was afraid, but straight away Foss came running up and he welcomed me and –' she looks at him – 'we became best friends.' She drops her white face for a moment and studies her paws.

Foss raises his nose. 'I was born here. I can trace my lineage back to the first settlers.'

'Oh!' says Roux.

'My great-grandfather was the first cat here, in 2001. His name was Chesterfield. He came with his brother, Herringbone, but we don't like to talk about *him*. Chesterfield was brought here by the men in gloves as a mouser. His wife, my great-grandmother, arrived in a skip, as did my grandmother and my mother.'

He looks for a moment at Sonata. Her two blue eyes meet his lonely one, before he blinks and looks away.

'Now it's your turn, Dew,' Sonata says, and all the cats look up at where Dew is sitting, but he is still distracted and doesn't seem to hear.

Just then there is a squawk, and Horatio lands high on a floodlight. 'They're coming,' he says, spreading his white wings wide, 'prepare yourselves. Starboard, cats, above the bins: two perpendicular columns. Quickly: action stations.'

Horatio's words have an electrifying effect on the cats, who spring as one from the ground to vantage points on bottle banks and green bins.

'Who's coming?' Malkin asks, jumping up on to Green Glass next to Foss. 'And what's that awful smell?'

'It is just a little matter, *chéri*,' Marmelade calls over. 'We are at war.'

'No time to explain now,' says Foss. 'Can you fight?' He turns his one eye briefly on Malkin, then back to the wall.

'I avoid violence.'

'You've lost that luxury. Here they come.'

And from over the wall that divides them pour the bodies of the Putrescibles.

Chapter 22

The Putrescibles

There are five of them, and they stink. Malkin finds himself trying not to breathe; the smell is so repulsive. Beside him, Foss hums with tension. Malkin lets out a shuddering breath, then inhales a long one. Foss flicks his amber eye to him to see if it means fear.

Malkin waves a paw in front of his nose to show it doesn't.

He looks over at Roux, standing on a bottle bank, and sees her body is taut, her tail high, and she is positioned slightly behind Sonata. She looks afraid, but her sixth is strong, as if she is almost ready to fight, but yet she is still more Domestic than Wild. Malkin wants to get over to her and looks for the best route, when Marmelade makes a wonderful leap and stands in front of her.

Marmelade looks over at Malkin and nods.

Malkin nods back, full of gratitude towards the blue cat.

The Putrescibles' lead cat is a dark tortoiseshell. He has a long wiry body that seems twice as long as a normal body, like a lorry Malkin once saw with a bend in the middle of it. He has slanted glistering yellow eyes, long whiskers that zigzag into the air and a wide smile that shows teeth as sharp as broken bottles. His pointed ears are perfect triangles.

He sits on his back two paws, raises his tail and does something that Malkin has never seen. He lets his claws out one by one, starting in his left paw, and finishing with the final claw on his right. Each makes a sound like wind on glass as it slices through the air, and each claw is twice as long as the claws poking from Malkin's own paws.

The cat grins during his orchestra of sound, looking up and holding the eye of Foss for each single claw. Malkin feels the anger humming from Foss, and his need to fight.

Malkin feels inside himself for fear, and finds it entirely missing. He remembers a wriggling bag, and freezing whooshing water, and paws that he tried to pull out of the water. He remembers the night when he nearly died, when his lives were ready to sink all in a line, and he remembers the mink that took away Roux's first life and the dog that he fought in the pub. He digs deep into those feelings and he looks at the exceptional claws of the cat and he thinks, *If I have to fight, I will fight, and I can fight hard. I can fight my own kind if it means keeping my friends and my wife safe.*

'You know what we've come for,' the lead cat says. 'We need a place to live, a place that is safe for our child.' His voice reminds Malkin of the lines through the sky where electricity flows that must never be touched. He feels a similar energy running through Foss, but it is Foss's right eye that is sealed shut, and Malkin is standing on Foss's right side so he can't read his face, only feel his sixth and see the way his fur bristles.

The four cats sitting behind the lead cat tilt their heads in unison. Two girl cats, two boys. All of them bone-thin.

'And you know we can't give up our home, Toxic.' That is Dew. He is nearer the ground than the others, standing on the low lid of Jars. His voice is calm after the hot metal whine of Toxic's voice.

The cat called Toxic moves forward. Behind him the two female cats weave to the left, where Marmelade, Sonata and Roux are waiting, and the two male cats weave to the right, the four of them in perfect synchrony.

All the cats on the ground tilt their heads upwards for a moment. The cats atop the bins hold still. There is a tense feeling in the air while every whisker is held upright

135

and every claw is ready to shoot out and slice. Malkin feels his sixth sense flash white, whizzing its way from his ears to his paws and up to the tip of his tail. Time stops moving. All is quiet.

Then Toxic lets out a cry.

The cats on the ground spring.

And everything is about sound and fury.

Toxic lands on Foss. He is upon him very suddenly, but Foss springs into being. He fights with the instincts of a tiger. Even though he is the smaller cat, his ferocity and quick, fearless moves make it look as if he will be the winner. But Malkin's observations are over in the matter of a moment because then a yellow cat lands on him and everything changes.

Malkin is shocked by the attack: the closeness of the stranger, the anger and hatred in the eyes that narrow before him. The fact that this cat, whom Malkin does not know, whom Malkin has not met, has never spoken to, that this cat could land on him, invade his space, and now raise his claws, ready to slice down on Malkin's face …

Malkin finds he can't breathe, but it isn't the cat pushing down on him, and he can't work out what it is until he realises it is the stink of the creature. So he chooses to turn off all his senses and just use his instinct: his sixth sense. The sense that never lets him down.

There is no smell. Everything becomes quiet. The furious noise of screaming cat and spit and scratch and the clawing against the metal of the bins stops.

Malkin focuses on the cat on top of him.

Malkin is pinned down on the soft part of his stomach, the gentle part, the part where food goes and the fur is not so thick and the blood beats close to the surface, and the weight of the stranger cat is on him and, any second now, he can sense the stranger cat is going to hit one paw down on his face, and rake down, and take away anything that is there, and leave just blood; while the other is going to pierce his stomach.

And surprise converts to anger.

Malkin is up and his magnificent tail is released and he throws the stranger cat from him in an instant. It is not difficult. In fact it is easy. And Malkin turns his sight back on and takes a moment to watch the surprise on the stranger cat's face as he begins his dizzying descent backwards through air to ground, and he almost turns on his hearing so he can listen to the shock, and then the appeal for help, and then the pain of the fall. He almost does, but there is something louder in his heart, that is distracting him from further protecting himself. It is flashing in his head and thrumming in his fur and electrifying his senses: it is the feeling Malkin loves, that makes him feel most himself – the feeling that someone needs his help.

He turns light and delicate and raises himself up, retracts and then extends his claws in mid-air, suspends himself for a split second, a second of watching to see where to position his weight, what angle to take, where to latch in to create most damage to the cat called Toxic and not to hurt Foss at all, because Foss is losing his fight. Foss is being held in those long razor claws and his white throat is bleeding, and he cannot move as the soft part of his throat is pinned by those claws. He has closed his one eye and turned his head to the left to shield it, and that is all he can do, the only thing he can do to protect his eye while the larger cat has all of him pinned. So Foss does not see Malkin elevated above him, and nor does Toxic.

Malkin can see Toxic saying words into Foss's exposed ear, and even without hearing the words, Malkin can sense the slow, soft threat of them, insidious and hateful.

And it is that sense of Foss needing his help that makes Malkin reconnect with gravity, so he falls, just so, eighteen claws full out, on to the stranger cat's back and pulls

him away. Malkin feels his claws contact fur, and slide through fur into soft skin, and the warmth of blood that comes with the slice of claw that Malkin has felt once before, and does not like, and yet he knows that he has to do this to save his friend.

The shock makes Toxic release his grasp of Foss and try to twist and turn on to his captor, but as he turns he exposes his soft side, and it is that side that Malkin goes for, straight to his throat and his stomach, not cutting into them, but pinning this cat down and getting him away from Foss. Foss who is lying there, barely moving, his paws clapped over his eye and the place where his other eye once was. He is shaking softly.

Now everything is about Toxic. Malkin finds himself up close to this cat that he does not know, that is nothing to do with his world, and he sees the wild fury in the yellow eyes and senses the mixture of pain and rage and a great deal of surprise.

The cat is speaking to him, saying something, but Malkin cannot hear and does not want to hear, does not want to find himself distracted.

Malkin cannot sense good in this cat. This cat had wanted to take away Foss's one remaining eye and leave him blind. Malkin raises his paw, his sharp claws exposed ... then, from the corner of his eye, he sees Roux jump. And this time he spins without hesitation to make sure she is not hurt, thinking at once how wrong he was not to look after her first and how if anything has happened ...

... but she is not hurt. She has jumped to the ground, and is looking up at him with concern, but she is safe.

Malkin turns back to the cat beneath him.

But something is wrong.

Something is terribly wrong.

Malkin watches horror spread across the cat's face, and feels it reflected in his own as he looks at his claw and realises with a feeling like cold water on warm fur what he has done: for stuck in his claw is the very tip that made the perfect triangle of Toxic's ear.

Malkin turns on all his senses in a flash as he tries to shake the tiny triangle of ear from the end of his claw.

Toxic yowls and howls in surprise, pain and perfect disbelief. He looks to retaliate, then reads something in Malkin that makes him spring from the bin and send a painful, piercing cry to the others.

At once all the cats stop fighting.

The pain in the cry rings around the bins a few times more: amplified by the bottles and jars.

Then all the enemy cats turn as one, the yellow cat limping at the back, and they follow Toxic, who has streamed like smoke back over the wall from whence he came.

Chapter 23
Territory

'How are you?' Sonata asks Foss, her voice weak with worry. But Foss has his one eye fixed on Malkin. Malkin looks away. The burden of what he has done is heavy on him. The tip of that cat's ear is gone forever.

'I think I'm OK,' Foss says quietly, although the holes in his neck where Toxic dug in his claws burn badly, as if they sting from more than just sharpness. He is wrapped in a knitted cardigan that Sonata has brought over from Mixed Textiles and Clothes.

Foss feels a churn of emotions: usually he loves to fight, is good at fighting, but Toxic has beaten him once again, has pinned him down, has whispered how he is going to take his other eye too. How the white girl cat will never look at him once he has no eyes, once he is blind and reliant on his friends to bring him food and help him.

142

With his one eye closed Foss had needed to arm himself with all his other senses; so he had been forced to listen to the *ting!* of each claw coming out in a slowly paced succession and had to feel those claws pushing into him, piercing and pinning him. He'd known that the inevitable was about to happen: one sense was going to be lost, the world was about to become dark, and then … not … then air and light and no more pain.

His tail twitches, his whiskers shake, a mew escapes him.

'He needs medicine,' says Sonata, watching the trembling course once again through her friend's striped fur. 'He's still in shock.'

'He needs the stuff that stings, on the cuts in his neck,' says Roux, leaning over. 'They look deep.'

'Don't worry, Foss darling,' Sonata whispers. 'I'll find you the stuff that stings. I'll be right back.'

But the *darling* has already taken half the pain away.

'Who were those cats?' Malkin asks as Sonata runs off.

'Those were the Putrescibles,' says Dew. 'They live on the other side of the great wall. This is what we were about to tell you: we were going to warn you, but then they came just before we had the chance. I'm sorry.'

143

'That's perfectly all right,' says Roux. 'We're fine, aren't we, Malkin?'

'Yes,' says Malkin, but he is thinking about the ear on his claw.

'The first cat you fought, Malkin, is called Yellow – he comes from a big city called London. You have to be careful of cats from big cities; they fight tough. The cat whose ear you took is called Toxic – he's the leader. The white girl cat is called Salt; she's married to him. The young boy cat is called Phobos – he's a good fighter and he's clever too. The albino cat is called Orchid. She doesn't come outside much, and never in the daytime; they bring her out when they want a big battle. She's not strong, but she is very, very brave.'

'The Putres– I find that a hard word to say,' Roux says.

'We all find that a hard word to say.' Foss's voice is bitter.

'Break it down, Roux: Put-resc-ibles,' Dew explains. 'It's *pute* – like a bit of a computer – or short for putrid – *ress*– the s is soft and mean, like a hiss, – *kibbles* – like kibble the hard food.'

'Ah! You make it sound like reading,' Roux says.

'Yes,' says Dew, and his eyes are bright. 'You know how to read?'

'Of course!' says Roux, 'I *love* reading, and Malkin is learning too; he's getting very good.'

'Books are one of the great joys of my life,' agrees Dew. 'I have created a small library over in Newspapers. It is a huge relief for me to hear we have two more readers here in our Recycling Centre home. When my final life goes ...'

'Oh, but don't say that, Dew! Please.'

'But why did the Putrescibles attack us?' Malkin asks, changing the subject.

'That's what the Putrescibles do,' Foss says. 'It all goes back to the argument Great-Grandfather Chesterfield had with his brother Herringbone, that sent Herringbone over the wall. Herringbone was the first Putrescible. Since the day his first kitten was born they have wanted to take over this side of the wall. They are prepared to kill for it.' And he rubs his neck with a striped paw.

'What's their side of the wall like?' Malkin asks.

'There's nothing good on their side, Malkin,' Dew says. 'Did you see how thin they are?'

'Yes, I did. It made me sad to see cats so hungry.'

Foss cuts in. 'Their side is disgusting. It's no place to live. It stinks. Smoke rises from the waste. Occasionally it catches fire. It's very dangerous.'

'It's a wasteland,' agrees Dew. 'It's where everything is thrown that is no good for humans and terrible for cats. The earth kills. It burns and hurts and makes you bleed. There is stuff over there that once you touch it you are bound to lose a life – perhaps even all your lives. There is so little to eat, and eating is a risk, because the food can be poisoned. The groundwater is not safe to drink as things that have spilled out of the rubbish flow into it.'

Malkin is quiet for a moment. Then he says softly, 'It must be very hard to be civilised if you have so little.'

'That is true, Malkin,' Dew says.

'So what happened between Chesterfield and Herringbone, if you don't mind my asking?'

'Chesterfield, my great-grandfather,' Foss says proudly, 'had an argument with his brother Herringbone. Herringbone was banished to the other side of the wall. One day a stray turned up on his side – she was a Domestic but her Owner had got very old and died. That was the start of the Putrescibles.'

'The stray was a beautiful black female cat called Molasses,' Dew continues. 'Herringbone and Molasses fell in love and started their own family on the other side of the wall, and on this side Foss's great-grandmother turned up in a rural skip full of recyclables for the Re-Use Shop, and they started a family here.'

'I'm so glad Herringbone was not on his own, and that the cats found love, but it's a terrible shame that there was the argument in the first place,' Malkin says. 'It's a shame that ever happened, and that it got so bad and no one just said sorry.'

'You are right, Malkin,' Dew says, 'but I'm afraid it's too late for sorry.'

'They used to keep to their side,' Foss says, 'but lately they've been invading us because they want to live over here. Toxic and Salt have had a kitten and it's changed things; they've become even fiercer. They're determined to drive us away and take over our territory.'

'But this side is enormous,' says Malkin, 'and I haven't even explored it all yet! Isn't there enough room for everyone to live over here? You've been so kind and said that Roux and I can stay – why can't the other cats move over too? Can't we all share?'

'Horatio told us you were good. He told us you saved his life on the beach. We knew you would be kind, be one of us,' Foss says, 'but the Putrescibles don't know how to share: they are fiercely territorial. They want this side to be their territory and no one else's. You must understand, if anyone goes over to their side they take lives. They want to drive us away. They want to live here alone. We cannot risk having anything to do with them; they are too dangerous.'

Foss closes his eye.

Malkin feels there is a secret waiting to be told. It makes his sixth sense tingle like a scratchless itch.

Then Foss speaks again. 'The night that Toxic took my eye,' he says, lifting his head slightly, 'that night …'

Dew picks up where he left off. 'We had a friend called Sage. Sage was always calm and he didn't like to fight. But after Sage saw what Toxic had done to Foss's eye, something snapped in his sixth, and he fought Toxic and beat him. Toxic went back over the wall …'

The cats look at each other.

'… and we thought he had gone. But while Sonata and I were taking care of Foss, Toxic came back. He found Sage where he was sleeping. And this time he had poison on his claws.'

Foss finishes the story. 'And three days later Sage lost five lives. They tumbled from him – like when the men in gloves empty the new glass delivery and all the bottles and jars smash beneath.'

'His lives all went in quick succession,' Sonata says.

'*All* his lives?' Roux asks.

'All his lives,' Foss says. 'He died. Sage died. Toxic killed him.'

Malkin jumps at a sudden sound, but it is just Marmelade returning.

'I was worried,' said Roux. 'You disappeared so quickly at the end of the fight. I thought Orchid might have hurt you. Thank you for looking after me.'

'*Ma chérie*, don't be ridiculous. I am a pure-blooded Chartreux. We are exceptional hunters. In France the farmers own Chartreux less noble than me to keep their farms clear from vermin. *Non, chérie*, I stank, it was disgusting. I felt sick. I had to go to wash myself in my basin.' There is an intake of breath, 'I know. I hate the water too, but I would rather lose a life than stink like that for a moment longer. Also, there is always the threat of fleas, where the Putrescibles are concerned.'

Roux scratches cautiously behind her ear, then sniffs the air. 'What is that smell?'

'It is not smell, *ma chérie*, it is fragrance. It is called Chanel No. 5 and it comes from France, like my ancestors. I found it in Glass Jars. I was keeping it in my armoire for an emergency. This was such an emergency. Even after I had my bath I still felt dirty, so I have used a little of the perfume.'

'Oh, the things people throw away,' Roux says wistfully, wishing she could ever smell so lovely. She looks over to Malkin, but he is rapt in thought and lost somewhere in his sixth sense, staring over at the great wall.

'Malkin?' she asks, and nudges him with her nose.

Malkin ruffles his fur and turns to her. 'Yes, Roux?'

'What are you thinking?'

'I'm thinking about the wall that divides us and I'm thinking about territory. Oh, Roux, I think it is up to me to create peace in this place. I know I have to unite all the cats, to do good for cat-kind. But for all the lives of me, I don't know how. I simply don't know. It feels too big.'

Chapter 24
Making Peace

Late the next afternoon, Malkin is walking through the Recycling Centre on his own while Roux is having high tea with Marmelade and Sonata in Small Domestic Items. He is thinking about the poor cats on the other side of the wall. The cats with so little. He thinks about their thin bodies and about the kittens they have and how dangerous it is for them where they live.

He thinks about what he said to the others about civilisation: *It's being kind to everyone. It's showing kindness to creatures who have less than you, even the ones who are unkind to you.*

Those words burn a small, bright flame inside his heart that he cannot hope to extinguish. If that is civilisation, then he has not been civilised. He thinks of the horror of the tip of the ear he has taken and remembers the sight of it stuck on his claw. How he had had to shake his paw more than once before the thing had been flung from him and on to the bin.

He mews for that ear and he wonders how he can make himself a better cat. The best cat he can be. A cat who is kind to everyone all the time, a cat who does the right thing in the wrong situation. Even during a fight.

Malkin is sitting in TVs/Computer Monitors, staring at a blank screen – his great tail slumped over the television he is sitting on – when Foss finds him.

'I wanted to say thank you, Malkin. For saving my eye. I should have yesterday, but I was feeling angry after the fight.'

'Don't mention it, Foss. Anyone would have done the same. How are you feeling today?'

'It still burns a bit –' Foss rubs a paw gently over the place where the fur has been torn away from his throat, leaving the flesh beneath exposed and red looking – 'and I felt a bit dizzy when I woke up. But it doesn't matter: I'd be blind without you.'

'And then you'd never be able to see Sonata again,' Malkin says quietly.

Foss darts a sharp amber look at Malkin and his

whiskers rise and his back arches. Then he slumps, and his nose points to the ground and he closes his one eye.

'Yes,' he admits.

The two cats sit in a heavy silence of their own creation and let it swoop and grow around them, eliminating the sounds of the centre: the machinery, the lorries beeping backwards, the moving sounds, the heavy sounds, the crushing sounds, a glass delivery being poured. All the loud sounds as they gently turn away from their sense of hearing and envelop themselves in silence.

'You can use your sixth sense to read me, if you like,' Malkin says. 'I'd like to get to know you better, Foss. It would be good to be friends.'

'Yes. It would be far easier if you read my sixth too,' says Foss. 'I don't think I have the words to explain my feelings out loud. It is better that you read them for yourself.'

So the cats shuffle close to one another and they each let their sixth sense read the other's feelings. And neither cat pushes the other out; rather they share their deepest, brightest secrets.

'You love her very much,' Malkin says finally.

Foss nods. 'Ever since I first laid eyes on her.'

'So why haven't you told her?'

'I was about to. It was a few months after she arrived at the centre. I was building up the courage to do it.'

'So what happened?'

'The fight. Toxic took my eye and I knew I never could. Not then, not after that.'

'But why?'

'Have you looked at Sonata, Malkin?'

'Of course I have. What do you mean?'

'So you have seen she is the most beautiful cat in the whole world.'

'Well ...' says Malkin, thinking of Roux, 'she is very pretty.'

'No, Malkin. She is beautiful. And what would a beautiful white cat, with two beautiful wide eyes, want with a one-eyed tabby like me?'

'Oh, Foss, don't say that! That's not how love works. Do you read Sonata's feelings? Using your sixth, I mean.'

Foss shakes his head. 'I turn off my sixth sense when she is near me. Always have done: first of all because I was shy, and then, after I lost my eye, because I knew it was foolish of me still to have love for her when there was no hope. She turns off her sixth too. I have never read her feelings and she hasn't read mine.'

154

'Have you ever wondered why she hides her feelings when she is around you?'

'Because she finds me horrid to look at, and frightening, and she is a kind cat and a beautiful cat and she knows to sense those things would hurt me.'

'Or,' says Malkin, 'it could be the other.'

'The other?'

'The opposite.'

'No,' Foss insists. 'She is as white, light and delicate as the flakes that fall from the sky on cold days. She has the moon inside her. Right in the hum and pulse and purr of her. Why would a beautiful cat like her look at someone like me? A cat with one eye.'

'Perhaps for love,' Malkin says.

'No,' Foss sighs, 'love is not possible for me. But today I feel better about that. For months I've thought that having one eye is a terrible thing, I've been so sad about it and so angry. But today I feel that having one eye is a wonderful thing. I could have had none. I am so grateful for my eye: I'm grateful to you. I just hope that one day I have the chance to repay you.'

'But you have seen what I want.'

'Yes,' says Foss, 'you want to create peace here. But I didn't need to read your sixth to know it. You are a

155

peacemaker. I can see it and sense it. And I can see that today you have slump in your tail because you are sad you took Toxic's ear.'

'I am, you are right, Foss. But the fighting – can't it end? We are all cats, we all live under the same moon. And … those cats over the wall … they are your relatives.'

Foss jumps and hisses. 'Don't say that. Don't *ever* say that. Herringbone was a disgrace to our family.'

'But what did he do? What did he say that was so bad?'

'No one remembers now, but it was bad.'

'This is what bad words do, Foss. When bad words are left in the air they start to pollute and poison and hurt all those around. The longer they are left the more hurtful they become, until all that is left is the hurt and no one can remember what started it. That is how poison works – you drop a little bit and it carries on spreading and hurting. I have seen poison left in bottles and spilling into the sea. I have seen what damage it can do.'

'It's not *us* who want to fight, Malkin, it's them. It will be worse now … after the ear.'

Malkin looks down at his paws. 'But what if we showed them kindness? If we used kind words.'

'Malkin. I have read your sixth and I know that you are very special, and I see the ring around your neck that means a moon present ... but I warn you. This is big. This is dangerous. Not everyone can be tamed by the promise of peace. Some creatures will agree to anything you say, then bite you anyway. Think about it. Now come on.'

'Where are you going?'

'It's Tuesday. We have to meet at midday. In Newspapers.'

'Why?'

'The local newspaper comes out each Monday and gets here on Tuesday. Dew reads it in the morning, then shares the important news with us at four thirtysharp. Dew loves reading. He told me he is very glad that you and Roux can read, so that when he is gone you will carry on teaching us.'

'That is a sad thought,' says Malkin. 'Which way is Newspapers?'

Foss holds up a striped paw and points diagonally across the centre. 'Across that way,' he says, 'not far from that end of the wall. There's lots to learn. Dew says books give you old knowledge – he's collected a small library of them – and newspapers tell you about the shifting, changing things around us. Some tell us about the wide,

wide world and some tell us about the town we're in and the things that are happening near us. Sometimes the news is close up – like the expansion of our Recycling Centre home – and sometimes it's about things that are happening across the sea. You'll like it.'

'It sounds very interesting,' Malkin says, feeling happier. 'Please show me the way.'

So the two cats jump down and head off.

Chapter 25
News Indeed

Dew is sitting on top of a big green bin under a sign that says 'Newspapers/Magazines/Books'. Under his front paws is a newspaper. When all the cats have arrived he holds up a paw.

'That means silence,' Sonata whispers to Roux, 'and we all have to sit nicely in a semicircle with our tails tucked in.'

The cats settle in a semicircle around Dew's bin. They wrap their tails neatly.

'Cats,' Dew says when they're settled, 'there is big news, medium news and little news. Which do you want first?'

'Little news,' calls out Marmelade. 'Make it small. *Petite.*'

'The little news is there is another Rural Skip Day next Thursday. It will pick up all the things for the Re-Use Shop from the villages along the Jurassic Coast.'

'And the other news?' Sonata calls.

'You are aware of the expansion of our centre near Entrance/Exit – depending on your point of view – by Paper Cups?'

'Yes,' Sonata says.

'They've finished it now. Our Recycling Centre home is expanded,' Dew says with some pride. 'We now aim to recycle ninety-five per cent of Devon's waste. It says the men in gloves are getting new lorries with seven compartments that the humans have to sort their rubbish into.'

'Is that the big news, Dew?' Marmelade asks, slightly disappointed.

'No,' says Dew, 'that is only medium news. There is big news. Very big news. News of the biggest kind.'

'Ooooooh,' breathe the cats, and they all tilt their ears forward. Dew opens the paper wide.

'Oh! That is a picture of our home!' shouts Marmelade. 'Look, there I am on my armoire! This is a very beautiful photograph. Look how I smile for the camera. Think how the humans will see me. The exact colour of my eyes! Turn over, Dew. Is there more?'

'Oh no! That's the other side of the wall. I think I see Toxic's tail sticking out from that container,' says Sonata. 'What's it about, Dew? What does it say?'

'PROTESTS ABOUT DANGER FROM LOCAL WASTELAND,' reads Dew.

'Good,' says Marmelade, 'the humans are protesting. This is very good news. This is the best news. They don't like the Putrescibles. They know they are dangerous.'

'It's not about the Putrescibles, Marmelade. It's about the waste.'

'The waste? What is happening, Dew?'

Dew coughs another little cough, then begins:

Residents of picturesque Starcross-on-Sea are mounting a protest against the stinking, putrid wasteland of rubbish known locally as Meeke Marshes that borders their Recycling Centre. Townspeople have long been campaigning to get the pile of waste removed.

Well known naturalist and local resident Dame Nora Andrews says, 'The council needs to take responsibility. We, as tax payers, demand that something is done about this blot on our landscape. There is a significant health risk for local residents from the toxins in the air and groundwater pollution.'

A spokesperson for the council said they are working with the Environment Agency to remove the waste and find a long-term solution to the problem. However, they could not state exactly when this will happen.

'That is not good enough,' said Dame Nora. 'This is why we are staging a protest at the town hall this Saturday. We urge local residents to come and make your voice heard. This tip must be cleared of rubbish and closed down.

'Hooray!' shout all the cats.

Their tails rise.

Marmelade breathes, 'Oh, *mon Dieu*. Oh, this is news. This is news indeed.'

And all the cats start talking at once.

'But,' Malkin says, 'if the humans do clear the other side of the wall, what will happen to the cats there? Where will they live?'

In all the excitement no one seems to hear him.

Chapter 26
The Kitten

Malkin has been worrying all the long afternoon and into the evening, when he hears the cries. They are tiny and high pitched, but in Malkin's ears they are quite loud enough.

The only problem is, they are coming from the other side of the wall.

Malkin pauses for a second, one paw lifted, nose to the wind and the inky blue of a sky that is turning to night. Then he feels the feeling he can't ever ignore – the pull to help someone. So it is without another thought that he scales the wall.

At the top he wrinkles his nose at the stench, looks down and feels his heart stop.

Foss, who is heading for supper in Aluminium and Steel Cans, senses his friend, and lifts his head just in time to see Malkin's tail disappearing over the top of the wall.

What? he thinks. *What am I seeing?*

Foss thinks he may be hallucinating, because he is still feeling unwell and there is a fire around his throat that is making his blood feel hot and his paws feel soft and slow. But he's sure that was Malkin's tail, and he knows Malkin is the sort of cat to cross the wall without considering the consequences.

Foss has to dig deep and remember his words: *I just hope that one day I have the chance to repay you.* His friend is in danger, and here is Foss's moment.

He shouts after Malkin, then thinks about going to call the others, but there is no time for that. Malkin is already over the wall.

Foss scrambles up. He has to use an ivy branch to help him, and it is with some difficulty, and a swoozy kind of dizziness, that he finally reaches the top.

Sitting on top of the wall makes his heart race. There is the Putrescibles' territory, as far as the eye can see: a mess of black bin bags and tyres and broken things and rotting meat bursting out of clear bags and bundles of the weeds that kill you if you eat them, and huge cans of acid spilling their remainders of clear liquid that burn and hurt your paws and change the colour of your fur even when your friends try to make you better. Once that stuff is on you it is over. Gas shoots from the ground in geysers. And through it all is Cats' Alley, the trench that leads to the place where the Putrescibles live and sleep.

As far as the horizon there is nothing of beauty, and it fills Foss with fear. He is so glad that he was born on the other side of the wall. He finds he is holding his breath against the noisome smell of it all.

Then he hears a high-pitched cry, and he looks down.

The kitten is tiny, small enough to hold in his paws. She should not be away from her mother. She is perhaps eight weeks old, no older than ten. Her bright blue eyes are open, peeping out from a mass of white fur, and she is mewing frantically because she is trapped, and tiny, and in pain and fear.

She is a kitten, but she is a Putrescible kitten, and Malkin is talking to her.

'Malkin! Malkin! What are you doing?'

Malkin looks up, then back to the kitten.

'Malkin, it's dangerous, you don't understand. They'll use the poison on you.'

Malkin can't think about that now. He has to help. He knows the men in gloves must not have seen the tiny kitten when they emptied out the rubbish skip. That they would have lifted it up high and then emptied the rubble and the broken paving slabs, tiles, bricks and concrete blocks in one long, loud crash. With all that sound and their feeble human ears they would not have heard the tiny kitten's cries of pain, but would have driven back across the wasteland away from the dust they'd created and the stench of the place.

Now the tiny kitten, finding herself stuck and afraid, is pulling and pulling to release her tail from beneath a sharp piece of broken paving slab and she is in very real danger of losing it forever.

Malkin whispers to her and tries to calm her. Then he tries to lift the slab, but it is too heavy for one cat. He feels that if he heaves with both front paws he may only succeed in lifting it for a moment before it comes crashing back down on the kitten.

He looks up to where Foss is waiting on the wall.

'It's now,' he says. 'This is the time to help.'

Foss is startled. This is not the help he'd expected to give. To jump, to deliberately jump, over to the other side of the wall – it is madness. It is a death sentence.

He shudders.

Then he looks down at his friend, struggling to help the kitten.

There is only one thing Foss can do.

'Here I go,' he says to himself. 'I must help my friend.' And he closes his eye, turns his sixth up sharp and jumps, landing dangerously close to a can with a poison sign on it.

'Help push,' says Malkin.

But Foss is in shock. 'I made it. I'm over. I did it, I jumped. I'm on the Other Side.'

'Thank you, Foss, now listen: the sooner you do this, the sooner you can get back over the wall. Help. Come on.'

Foss shakes himself, then gets his front paws under the slab. Together the two cats push and lift it up – enough to release the tail – but the kitten doesn't move.

'Move,' says Foss to the kitten. 'Move your tail.'

But the kitten is young, and in shock, and her blue eyes gaze at him without understanding.

'Do you think you can support the slab, just for a second?' Malkin asks. Already the strain of the weight is showing on Foss's face and his eye looks bleary.

'I can.'

'Right. I'm going to let go after five. Just hold it up for one more second. I just need one second.'

'Right.'

168

'One … two … three… four … five.'

Malkin bounces back and Foss has to support the full
weight of the slab by himself. In a single swoop Malkin
reaches down, bites the scruff of the kitten's neck and
pulls her out of harm's way, just as Foss loses his strength
and drops the sharp triangle of paving stone back down
with a crash.

Dust rises up as the stone cracks into two smaller
triangles.

Foss lies on the ground. His stomach is rising and
falling with the strain.

Malkin looks at the little bundle. She has stopped
crying now, but her beautiful blue eyes are closed.

Foss struggles to his paws. 'Need to go back over,' he
says. 'Come on. They'll have smelled us by now; they'll
be coming down Cats' Alley.'

'What's Cats' Alley?'

'That trench through the mud there. It leads to their home, whatever it is they live and sleep in. It's not real mud – it hasn't rained in days – but it's always wet along there. None of our side has ever been down it. Come on, Malkin. We shouldn't be here.'

'No,' says Malkin. 'She's in shock and I think her tail is broken.' The kitten is lying very still. 'You jump back over. I'm going to carry her to her mother.'

'Now you're just being crazy.'

'I'll watch you safely up the wall.'

'For the love of the moon, Malkin, please come.'

'Foss, you've helped me, and I thank you. Now you must go.'

Foss doesn't need telling again. He turns and scrabbles up the wall. He makes an awkward job of it and keeps slipping, as his head is dizzier than before. Finally he hauls himself to the top using the ivy.

He looks down at his friend. He tries one more time, 'Come up, Malkin. Please.'

'I can't. I have to do this.'

'You mustn't. It's madness.'

'Perhaps,' says Malkin, 'but it is the right thing to do.'

And with that he picks the kitten back up as gently

as he can, and, with her dangling against his chest, and her faint heartbeat throbbing in his mouth, he begins to pick his way through the stench of rotting rubbish towards the trench called Cats' Alley, being careful not to tread on the poison that leaks out of the cans and burns the paws.

Chapter 27

Revenge

Malkin picks his way over shattered fluorescent tubes, broken bags of butchers' waste, upturned bottles of bleach and a newly dead animal that the crows are picking at. They eye him but do not fly away. The stench of rotting meat and the hum of flies is all around and a wind is picking up that makes it all worse.

His paws have started to burn from something he has trodden in, that was cold and good when his paws first touched it but now is hurting very badly. He can smell the smell they used to clean the pub with in the early morning, when the human pushed around a yellow bucket and stood yellow triangles on the floor. It is the smell that Roux has warned him never to step in.

He must have stepped in it, because the smell is following him everywhere; it has become part of his own smell, part of him.

Now he is inside Cats' Alley. The trench is mainly clear, although there are sections where the men in gloves have dumped new waste on the boundary and it has spilled over. Malkin imagines how difficult it must be to try to keep the alley clear of rubbish. Like fighting a losing battle. No cat should have to live like this.

The little kitten's body in his mouth moves backwards and forwards, her legs dangling down, and he has to be soft in his footfalls so as not to hurt her more than she is hurt already.

Malkin feels danger everywhere. He cannot see what is at his feet and also keep his eyes fixed ahead, and he needs to keep his eyes fixed ahead as, among all the different smells, his nose has picked up what his nose was made to do: and he can smell the distinctive odour of the Putrescibles. He knows that if he is coming close to their home, they can, of course, smell him too.

Just then there is a wail, and the next moment the female white cat called Salt is springing through the air towards him. With the kitten in his mouth he can't spring, or pounce, or use his great tail to lift himself up, or do any of the things that he does so well. Instead he has to stand still, with the little bundle held in his mouth, waiting for the shock of the impact. He can't let the kitten fall, she is

173

too weak; instead he raises his front two paws to protect her and balances on his back legs.

Malkin feels the sharp sinking in of claws, to the left and right of his eyes, as the impact of the white cat falls full against his face. He feels the claws dig in and find the streams of blood beside his eyes. He feels a furious yank as Salt hacks her claws back out and pins him down, pushing him into the squashy ground.

'Give me my baby,' she hisses. 'Give her to me now.'

Malkin opens his mouth, and releases the kitten, which falls on to the safe softness of the white ruffle of his neck fur but makes no sound.

Salt falls to her knees and nudges her kitten with her nose, feeling for her heartbeat. She lets out a mew, then another, and the kitten utters a faint, painful cry. Malkin turns his head away; he chooses not to see Salt's sorrow.

Then the white cat snaps her attention back to him. 'There will be revenge for this,' she says, hissing a final hiss before scooping her precious child into her mouth and padding off, crying a terrible sound, one that fills Malkin with fear, not for him, but for a mother's breaking heart, because her kitten has lost a life.

He struggles to his feet, shakes out his fur, and turns back in the direction of the wall. He is bleeding, and he stinks, and he is pretty sure he will have more scars now, but he is alive and the kitten still has eight lives and the best chance of survival that he could give her.

He lifts a paw and stretches it out, but it doesn't move.

He tries again.

No motion. Just a tug on his tail.

Something is standing on it.

'And where do you think you're going?' says a voice like breaking glass.

And Malkin turns to face Toxic.

Chapter 28
Foss

Dew is pacing up and down as the girl cats begin to feel the strengthening in their claws that pulls them to their night's hunting.

'It's going to be a windy night,' says Marmelade, watching a fat plastic bag rustle by.

'Oh, where can Foss be?' asks Sonata. 'I've not seen him for hours and he needs more of the stuff that stings on his neck. I am worried; it's not getting better.' By her paw is the lid of a jar in which shimmers the stuff that stings. It took Sonata a very long time to find it at the bottom of a brown bottle, although she will not tell Foss that.

'I'm *so* worried about Malkin,' says Roux. 'It's not like him to go away for this long without telling me. I can't *think* what he's doing.'

There is a movement in the shadows. '*Alors*, here is Foss,' says Marmelade. 'About time.'

But something is wrong. Foss is moving slowly, dragging his paws, and, as he tries to make it on to the wine crate, he slumps to the ground instead. Sonata lets out a loud mew and springs to his side. Foss pulls himself into the narrow space between the crate and the box next to it, where it is dark and the walls are tight. He pulls his tail in and wraps it around himself as best he can and gives in to the shivers.

Sonata lets out a wail.

'Step back,' says Dew, appearing from nowhere and placing a paw on Foss's forehead.

'What is it?' asks Sonata.

'He's got a fever,' says Dew.

'It is not good for a cat to have a fever,' says Marmelade. 'It is never good.'

'He has hot and cold,' says Sonata. 'Quick, the stuff that stings – I will put it on him.'

'He's saying something.' Roux leans in closer to listen.

Foss's voice is very tiny indeed, more about breathing out than making any word sounds, and the cats have to hold their own breath to catch it: 'Malkin,' exhales Foss, 'he's gone over the wall.'

Roux lets out a cry. 'Oh no! Oh, *Malkin*! But we must go then. We must help him.'

'Yes, we must,' says Dew.

'*Sacré bleu*, what is wrong with your husband? Why would he do something like that? He wants to die, does he? But I am unafraid; I am made to fight. It is in my blood.'

'Yes, Marmelade, Dew, let's go,' says Roux, her claws coming out. 'I have eight lives. Quickly, everyone, we *must* go. Come on, Sonata.'

'I'm coming,' Sonata calls into the darkness. 'Wait for me.'

'Hurry,' says Roux. 'We'll wait on top of the wall. Oh, please, *do* be quick.'

Sonata looks at the curled-up figure of Foss on the ground. 'We won't be long. Just …' And she finds that she has no words, and her voice is coming out in strange mews, so she holds up one paw and softly strokes its pad over Foss's forehead.

His eye flickers open and he looks at her.

Then it closes again. Deep down in the place that Foss is falling to, he thinks Sonata's face is an effect of the fever. He thinks he has begun to dream.

A big shudder runs through his body.

Sonata sees it and a mew escapes her. 'Back soon,' she whispers into his ear. She dabs a paw in the stuff that stings and pads it on to his neck, where the fur is gone.

He doesn't even flinch.

She puts her nose close to his and she breathes him in. His little breaths are coming quickly and in shudders, as if pain has a hold of his insides.

He doesn't smell like himself.

That makes her afraid.

'Back soon,' she says again, 'my darling,' she adds.

She turns away, feeling a tearing in her soul, and leaps into the darkness where her friends are waiting for her on top of the wall.

Foss never hears that *darling*; he is looking at the face of the mother and father who made him, faces he has not seen for three years. They are smiling and purring. Behind them the moon shines strong, and it is the time of night when there is hunting to be done. All of a sudden he feels warm. He will be safe if he goes to them.

He leaps towards the moon.

Between the crate and the box, the tip of Foss's tail flicks and the tips of his ears flick, and then he is quite, quite still.

Chapter 29

An Eye for an Ear

Malkin looks at the jagged shape where the perfect triangle of Toxic's ear had been. He doesn't watch each claw ping out, one at a time, because he doesn't want to. But he hears them, nevertheless, because the dark amplifies sounds and makes them more truthful.

'It's not what you think.'

'You've hurt my child and you want to tell me what to think.'

'That's not what happened.'

'And you expect me to listen to you? Be quiet, cat. You took my ear and you dared come over to our side of the wall to try to kill my Calica. And now you will pay for that.'

A little bit of blood drips into Malkin's right eye. He had forgotten he was injured. Now he feels the sharp pain of the deep scratches on his face while half the world becomes blood red. He doesn't want to fight.

'You took my ear,' says Toxic, on the ninth ping, 'and so I will take your eye.'

'I am sorry I took your ear,' Malkin says, 'but please don't make me take the other one.'

Toxic laughs, and it is like the cry of war that rattles the world all around. The sound that makes humans shudder and close their eyes and think, *Now things change.* 'The other one? Black cat, you have some confidence.'

'If you always take an eye for revenge, the whole Recycling Centre will end up blind.'

'So be it. If that is the way.'

Malkin closes his eyes and readies his body for Toxic's pounce.

It comes. Hitting him deep into the squelchy ground.

He remembers in that second being a kitten, washed up on a muddy bank, freezing and cold and close to death. He feels the cold, wet feeling that he hates so much. It makes him want to curl up and shiver the night through until dawn breaks and Roux will come to rescue him and his life will be new.

Next he feels those long, sharp claws, holding his throat, pinning him down. Pinning him, but not quite tearing him.

Still he does not want to fight.

He could fight and he could win again. He knows that. He won last time and now, with the missing part of his ear, Toxic will have lost a degree of balance.

But he doesn't want to. The horror of that ear between his claws haunts him.

And he knows his destiny. He is sure that the moon means for him to create peace in this place.

And so he will not fight.

The first of Toxic's claws digs in and draws blood. Malkin feels the sharpness of it inside the softness of his fur and the warm beat of his veins and the alien strangeness of the claw pressing in and releasing what should be kept inside.

Yet still he does not fight back.

He looks up, past the imperfect silhouette of Toxic's face. All around is the dark and the cold pressing against his eyes and his nose and his pads, until Toxic strikes him sideways and brings him face down into the squelch. Malkin would have sighed, but then his nose would have been full of the stench, so instead he turns off some senses, which is a relief, to blink away the last trace of blood from his eye, to get rid of the stink in his nose. He keeps hearing, and lets his body flood with his sixth. Toxic, who is now on his back, feels the flow of it, the tensing of the muscles, and the power within the young cat.

For a moment Toxic is afraid, and Malkin uses that moment to throw the cat from his back. Then there is the clear voice of Salt.

'What are you waiting for?' she screeches. She flies at Malkin's throat, grabs his fur and rips a chunk of his moon ring away.

Malkin falls backwards, and as he falls he smells his favourite smell in the world. The smell he would know anywhere. Because even in the stink of this place, even in all the bad, Malkin knows that beauty is stronger.

That it is always stronger, and sometimes harder, but it is always right to be good.

And the smell is good. It is very good: wet grass and small flowers. It is exactly what Cats' Alley needs.

But he doesn't want her to walk into this danger.

'Roux!' Malkin shouts. 'Are you here?'

'The cat is mad,' says Salt. 'He's hearing things.' Yet still she raises her nose and inhales some seconds of the night air. 'Toxic! I smell something, something sweet is coming.'

'No, Salt. That's just the wind from the other side. It's only us here,' Toxic hisses, his wide yellow eyes flashing. And he pushes a sharp, double-length claw into the soft fur around Malkin's neck. 'You're on your own, black cat,' he whispers into the ear he is going to take any moment now, right after he rips away the rest of the moon ring that protects his enemy's throat.

'No, he's not,' says Roux.

Toxic and Salt look up.

'We're here,' Roux says, and the scratch in her voice says she is ready to fight, 'Now get *off* my husband.'

Behind her stand the figures of Dew, Marmelade and Sonata.

Five against two is not good odds.

'Run,' says Malkin.

'Or stay and die,' says Marmelade, waggling the claws that have sprung from her paw pads. 'It is a simple choice, even for a Putrescible.'

Toxic and Salt look at each other for the briefest of moments, then spring around and run back down Cats' Alley.

Chapter 30
Blue Cross

When the cats return Sonata immediately crawls into Foss's space with him. Then she lets out a terrible cry, 'He's lost a life! Oh no! He's lost a life. He's down to five. I wasn't even here to hold him!'

The cats looks at each other as Sonata curls herself around Foss, whispering his name. He does not open his eye. His paws move limply and there is too much heat in him. Worst of all, he smells funny. He almost smells like a Putrescible.

Sonata keeps her paws around him.

The wind picks up, sending paper and cardboard tumbling by. A few drops of rain begin to fall and make their strange music around the centre.

The cats take shelter under the crates and boxes nearest to Foss, calling across the space to one another.

'Will he lose all five?' Marmelade calls. 'This is a very

bad fever that he has. Perhaps all his lives will go quickly, one after the other, like with Sage.'

'Marmelade!' warns Dew. 'Don't speak like that. I don't know what to do. He needs medicine that we can't provide.'

'Well, *I* know what we must do, Sonata,' says Marmelade, raising her voice against the wind and rain, 'but you won't like to hear it, *chérie*.'

'What?' calls Sonata. 'What can we do?'

'We must let the Blue Cross people have him. It is the only way.'

'Absolutely not.'

'Why not, *chérie*, if it is his chance to survive?'

'Because then I will have lost him forever. It was bad enough after the terrible fight that changed everything. We were so close to love. We were almost there, but then he lost his eye and I lost his heart. I was so sad, but at least I still had him here. It was enough for me. Almost enough. Please don't take him from me.'

'But, *chérie*, if we take him near the men with gloves, they will see that he is ill. They will call the Blue Cross woman with the hoop who drives the van. They have vets at this Blue Cross.'

'Foss doesn't need a vet,' Sonata says. 'He needs rest and love and the stuff that stings.'

'He needs more than that now,' Dew says gently, tripping lightly through the rain to the space by the crate and looking in. 'Marmelade is right – he needs to see a vet. The poison has been in his blood for some time. He is getting worse.'

'He has no poison in his blood.' Sonata's voice is high. 'How would he have got poison in his blood?'

'Toxic. Toxic had it on his claws.'

'If Toxic had poison on his claws, Malkin would be ill as well. Malkin fought Toxic that night – he took his ear, remember? And he hasn't got a fever.'

'The time I took Toxic's ear he didn't scratch me,' calls Malkin from the box he is sheltering in. 'Not that time – not the time he hurt Foss; he didn't get the chance.'

'But he scratched you just now.'

'That's true. My wounds hurt, but they don't burn.'

'Foss isn't leaving me,' Sonata says, 'and that's final.'

'We have to take him to the men in gloves, *chérie*. They are the only ones who can help him now. We need human help. They'll get the Blue Cross people.'

'But I'll never see him again.'

'No, you won't,' says Marmelade, 'but that is *amour*, that is the nature of the thing. You have to lose love, sometimes, in order to win love. Dew has read me stories of this.'

'I can't.'

'*Oui*, Sonata, it is true that you can't, and yet you know that you have to. You must prepare yourself, Sonata, you may have to say *adieu*, as my ancestors said in France. Not *au revoir*.'

Sonata begins to wail.

'Please agree, Sonata,' Dew says. 'For Foss.'

Sonata crawls around in the narrow space, her back to Dew, her body hunched over Foss.

She cries softly for a while, and then she falls silent and her silence stretches around them all.

'Very well,' she says finally. 'If he isn't better by midday tomorrow we will take him to the men with gloves. They can get the Blue Cross. Then the rest of you keep clear. You don't want them to take you too.'

She hunkers further into the narrow space, winds herself as close as can be to Foss's shuddering body, and closes her eyes.

Chapter 31

Honour

'It is time,' says Marmelade at midday. 'We must take him. I have been to see where the men in gloves are. We will carry Foss there and then leave him. The men in gloves will help him, *chérie*, they will call the Blue Cross as they have done for us before.'

'I think he's a little better,' says Sonata. 'I think we should wait; a bit longer, that's all.'

'It is time,' says Malkin, 'like Marmelade said. Let's take him. Be brave, Sonata.'

'We will all be with you,' says Roux. 'We will stay with you until he is taken …' But then her voice fails as she feels a sense of Sonata's loneliness without her Foss.

It is then that Toxic and Salt land on the wall.

All the cats smell and sense them at the same time and their heads rise in unison.

Toxic has a green plant with purple flowers hanging

from his mouth. It is a big plant, so Malkin can hardly see the cat behind it.

'What do you want?' hisses Sonata, curving herself into an S. 'Don't you think you've done enough?'

Salt blinks slowly and looks at Malkin. 'We have something to say to you, black cat, and to your friend here who is ill.'

'Very well,' says Malkin.

191

'Calica is no longer in shock. Her first words were about you. She said you and your friend saved her. We didn't know, and we're sorry. Aren't we, Toxic?'

The plant goes up and down as Toxic nods.

'Calica explained she was trapped by her tail and you and your friend got her out – this one here who is ill. You saved my baby's life. We wish to repay you, and we can: we know why your friend is ill.'

'Go away,' hisses Sonata. 'So do we. We know *perfectly* well why Foss is ill, and that is why we want *nothing* from you.'

'Give them a chance, Sonata,' says Malkin. 'They've come to help Foss. Perhaps they can save him.'

And Sonata hisses, but does not speak.

'You seem to think we have no honour, but we do have honour,' Salt continues, raising her nose. 'We will not allow a debt to go unpaid. All we want is for you to be fair about your land and provide a safe place for us to live and raise our kitten. But in the meantime we have brought this plant for your friend Foss here. If you grant us permission to cross the wall.'

'It's a trick,' says Marmelade. 'Do not trust them. Look at them. And if you can't look –' she wrinkles up her tiny blue nose – 'smell.'

'It's five against two,' says Dew. 'If they've come to fight, the odds are in our favour.'

'Not if he has that poison on his claws again,' says Sonata. 'Not with cats who don't fight fair.'

'Give them a chance,' says Malkin. 'We are all cat-kind. We are all the same – it's just our circumstances that are different. Marmelade, you think that because where they live is dirty and smelly it makes them disgusting. Well, I have been kept locked in a barn. Does that make me a bad cat?'

'I think you should listen to Malkin,' Roux says quietly.

'These bad words go back to a bad argument. And this is what happens with bad words – they go on and on until no one remembers what they were, but everyone lives with the consequences. But, goodness, once that starts, it never stops. If you keep being good, then those around you become good too. And everyone is far happier. The first step is trust. If you cannot trust them to come over here and help you, Sonata, then you will lose your Foss, and then you will be even more angry with them and so it will go on. But if you trust them …'

Sonata looks at Foss, who has started to shiver. 'Very well,' she says. 'They can bring the plant.'

Toxic jumps down, followed by Salt. He walks to

where Foss is lying and drops the green plant with the purple flowers. It smells strange. Marmelade turns her nose away.

Toxic sits on his two back paws. 'That plant,' he says, 'will make your friend better.'

Dew pads the plant with his paw. 'I have read about a plant with green leaves and purple flowers,' he says. 'They are telling the truth, Sonata. It is one of the plants cats can use to heal themselves.'

'The plant is bad for humans so it's dumped on our side of the wall. But it's good for cats,' Salt says. 'You must rub a little into his wounds and mix a little in water. Get him to drink it, or put it on his nose. We have been using the plant for a long time, because we often get the bad stuff in our blood. We store it every time it is dumped. It makes you better very quickly.'

'Then we thank you,' says Malkin.

'We do not!' says Sonata. 'You put poison on your claws and you killed Sage and now you've hurt Foss.' Her words are strong, but her voice trembles; and a mew comes out at the end.

The zigzag of Toxic's whiskers droops. 'That was an accident,' he says. 'There's so much bad stuff on our side. My claws are very long –' he picks up one front paw – 'it gets in them. I'm sorry for your friend Sage: he was always gentle and kind. That night I came back over to see if he was getting better: I was worried I had hurt him very badly. I didn't hurt him again that night, but I am afraid the damage was already done. And I'm sorry now about Foss's eye, that I took it, that time. It was very kind of him to help Calica, and I see the strain has made him ill.'

The two white female cats stare at each other for a moment. Then Sonata hisses and raises her tail.

Salt turns and takes a great leap on to the wall. Toxic springs up beside her.

Then the two cats jump over without looking back.

The second they are gone Sonata begins to tear at the plant with her claws and teeth. Roux helps mix it in fresh rainwater.

They dap it gently on Foss's wounds and on his nose.

Then they wait.

After a while his paws twitch.

Sonata takes a sharp breath. 'Foss? Foss, I'm here. It's Sonata. I'm holding you, I promise. You can let go now, let that old life go, there's another one waiting right here for you, and it is going to be …' But she has to stop talking for a moment because her lovely soft voice is broken.

'I am going to *make sure* that your next life is perfect. Let go now, I've got you, I'll catch you.'

Deep, deep inside, Foss hears Sonata's voice.

Yes, he thinks, *that is her. That is the cat that I love.*

So Foss lets go of another life.

Inside him there is a *whoosh* of the brightest, lightest colours, and all the good feelings: from his earliest memories of his parents raising him in the Recycling Centre, to the day that Sonata arrived in a skip, just like his mother, and his grandmother, and his great-grandmother before her, to making friends with the other cats. The feeling of hunting is there too, and seeing the world through two eyes.

'I've got you, darling.'

It's her voice again. It floods his senses. The strange feeling begins to let go. The dreams ebb away and the heavy, heavy tug of gravity is there.

Foss says goodbye to his mother and father and he turns from the moon, remembering something he's forgotten. The most important thing in the world.

Sonata puts her paws around him to carry him through the weightless feeling of losing a life.

He lets go of the life and then Foss feels himself again, but fresher, and better. He opens his eye, and finds bright blue eyes looking down at him and white paws holding him.

'Oh, Foss,' Sonata says, 'I thought I was going to lose you.'

Then she sits on her back paws and she covers her face and she cries. And Foss looks at her sorrow, all that sorrow for him, and he draws deeply on the brave cat he used to be and he does the only thing he can do.

He gets up, and he puts his paws tightly around Sonata, and he pulls her close.

'You are never going to lose me,' he says. 'Never.'

Chapter 32

Rain

That moon passes into the next, and then the next moon follows, and Roux and Malkin become very happy in their new home. Foss and Sonata are together all the time now, touching paws and noses a lot. Horatio often visits with news of the sea and the river and old friends. The men in gloves get new lorries with seven different compartments along the sides. They are very pleased and proud. All the cats are cheered by the good mood around them, and what makes it even better is they do not see the Putrescibles, who have been keeping to their side of the wall since the day they bought the plant for Foss.

But then, one morning, the sky is dark and it begins to pour with rain, and the cats' ears slump forward. They eat breakfast in Aluminium and Steel Cans which has just had a delivery. There is a lot of fresh food, but it does not cheer the mood of the cats. Even the men in gloves look fed up. The Recycling Centre is quiet, with just the sound of rain all around as it plinks against metal and glass.

'So that was what you English call summer,' says Marmelade, 'and now it will rain for nine months. If you need me, I will be resting under my armoire.'

'Oh, Malkin, I *do* hate the rain. I'm going to go to Dew's library to share books with Sonata,' Roux says.

But Malkin's nose is raised and he appears to be watching the wind shaking the blue netting above the neatly crushed and compacted cubes of drinks cans.

'Goodbye,' he says absently as he watches the cats run off. There is a feeling growing inside him. A feeling he has not felt in such a long time. It is the feeling that some-one needs his help. The feeling that makes him feel perfectly himself, perfectly right.

Malkin picks up his paws and runs into the rain. His sixth sense is pulling him towards Glass Bottles and Jars, and as he approaches he hears the clinking, clanking sound of glass being turned inside the huge new blue bin called Glass One, but there isn't a man in gloves in sight.

Then a ripped ear appears.

'Toxic!'

'Black cat.'

'Please call me Malkin. What are you doing here?'

'Go away,' says Toxic, but he neither springs to attack Malkin, nor does he move away.

Malkin approaches him slowly, and Toxic makes an *S* of his long back, and his zigzag whiskers stick right up, but his mouth is a straight line and his eyes close in pain.

'What's wrong, Toxic?'

Toxic's ears droop forward, and in the next second he slumps down. 'I'm trapped.'

'How?'

'I was looking for food when they poured more glass in. I crawled into the corner, but something sharp has landed on my back paw and it hurts very badly if I move it.'

'Keep still,' says Malkin, and he sticks his tail up, takes a great leap and lands in the bin.

'I see it,' he says. 'Oh dear. You've cut yourself and you're bleeding. Don't move. It's a broken jar and your paw is inside it and there's more on top of that. I can reach it. Stay really still.' And Malkin carefully lifts the glass away, then frees Toxic's paw.

Toxic looks long and hard at Malkin. 'Thank you,' he says finally. 'Now I will return to my side of the wall.'

'No,' says Malkin. 'Your paw is cut and bleeding and

you will need the stuff that stings. And there's something else … if you don't mind my saying.'

'What?'

'You are so thin. Thinner than ever.'

Toxic hangs his head again. 'We have a bad gas on our side called methane. Some rubbish caught fire, so the men in gloves came and put a thin layer of soil over everything. Now there is nothing to eat. Everything is covered. Hunger is everywhere.'

'But that's terrible. We have so much. Please let me help you.'

'No.'

'Then let me help your friends and your family.'

Toxic looks up. 'Very well,' he says at last.

'First I am going to fetch the stuff that stings for your paw and some cloth from Mixed Textiles to bandage it. Then we will find food and you can invite the others over to eat while I keep watch.'

'Your friends will attack us if they see us, and we are too weak to fight.'

'They won't. They're sheltering from the rain. And afterwards I will call a meeting in TVs and Monitors. It's right over the other side of the centre; you will be safe to come over and eat.'

* * *

After the two cats have gathered plenty of good food and left it hidden by the wall, Malkin looks closely at Toxic.

'Goodbye, my friend,' he says.

'Goodbye, Malkin. But, please, if you see me again, pretend this didn't happen.'

'Why?'

'It's for the best. In a different world, in different circumstances, we could have met and become friends, and I would have liked that very much. But this is war, and one day I may have to take one of your lives. It is easier for me to do that if we are not friends.'

'But it's stronger to have friends than enemies. Enemies only want to make your life bad. Choosing to be enemies is like choosing all the bad smells and flavours for your whole nine lives. Why would any cat do that?'

'We never wanted a war, but all of us were born into one. My daughter Calica will never know how plentiful life can be, but her mother and I let her believe that our side of the wall is good.' Toxic raises his twisted whiskers. 'That is why we were fighting: we wanted a better life for our daughter. But after you saved her we were in your debt, so we will no longer come here to fight.'

'I'm glad because I'm your friend. Even if one day you have to take one of my lives, you will still be my friend. That is not going to change. You do not have to say you're my friend in return, but you cannot stop me being yours. Now go, and I will round up the others on the far side of the centre. Each day I will leave some food in this exact place. Please come over to eat it.'

'Thank you, Malkin.'

And with that Malkin Moonlight watches his friend Toxic disappear like smoke over the wall that divides them.

Chapter 33

Big News

One afternoon a leaf blows and sticks itself on to Malkin's nose. Roux laughs, and bats the leaf away.

'The air smells different today, Malkin, don't you think? Like wet leaves and cold paws and excitement,' she says.

'Yes, it does,' agrees Malkin, 'but what does it mean? I've never smelled this smell before.'

'Autumn is here,' says Sonata with a smile. 'Soon it will be the harvest moon that is the same colour as Foss. Then November will come and the night when animals are afraid. When there are bangs and explosions and the sky lights up with fire and colours. It is something the humans do.'

'The sounds are very worrying for animals,' says Marmelade. 'They remind our sixth senses of all the bad things that can happen. Deep down we all have memories of these things. It is passed on through cat-kind. It is not a good night for cats.'

'It does sound *horrible*,' says Roux.

'It is,' agrees Foss. 'We will hide in cardboard boxes that night, like we did last year. We will feel safer there.'

'Yes,' says Sonata.

'Agreed,' says Malkin, but secretly he thinks he might leave his cardboard box just to have a look at the night sky being lit up with colours.

It is a Tuesday and the cats are making their way to Newspapers. When they arrive they sit nicely on the ground and look up at Dew.

Dew is looking very serious.

'There is big news today. The very biggest.'

'Oh,' say the cats, and tip their ears forward.

'WASTELAND TO BE CHANGED TO NATURE PARK!' Dew announces, then holds up the newspaper.

'Oh!' all the cats gasp.

'Look, Foss! I can see you peeking out of that box,' says Sonata. 'And there's the important man in gloves called the Site Manager.'

'He looks very smart in this photo. He is not wearing his orange clothes,' Marmelade says.

'What does it mean, Dew?' asks Malkin. 'What's the story about? Is it good news?'

'It is the very best news.' Dew gives a little cough and begins to read:

Meeke Marshes rubbish tip, which borders the Starcross-on-Sea Recycling Centre, is to be transformed into a thriving green space in a brand new environmental rehabilitation project. Local residents, including well known naturalist Dame Nora Andrews, have been calling for the tip to be reclaimed as green space. Architects' plans – see pages 4 and 5 – include a bird-watching paradise with footpaths and an arboretum. Work will begin shortly on the project, which has been granted a ten-million-pound environmental green certificate award. Site Manager Jerry Martin said, 'Plans are underway for diggers to clear the land and remove all existing waste to landfill. The land will then be flattened, filled and covered in clay and topsoil. Then the planting will take place. It is estimated that the nature park will be thriving within fifteen years. This is a great outcome for the local community.'

'Hooray!' say the cats, and their tails lift up.

'Diggers?' says Malkin, and Roux puts a paw on his. 'What about the cats on the other side?'

206

'Don't worry, Malkin,' Dew says. 'When the humans see the Putrescibles they will call the Blue Cross and they will be caught and re-homed.'

'But what if they don't see them, what with all the noise and rubbish being dug up? What if they don't see them at all? Or, if they do, what if they are not re-homed together: what if the Blue Cross put them in different homes?' And Malkin thinks of how it hurt to be away from Roux for just half a moon. And he thinks of Toxic and Salt looking at their kitten Calica for the final time. He imagines Calica being lifted up in gentle hands and taken from her mother and father. Calica who has never had an Owner and has always lived in a Wild community.

Inside Malkin everything shatters into pieces that feel small and sharp and flood his senses with darkness.

Then, in the next second, a small seed lands in all that dark. The seed of an idea. He looks around at his friends, and he knows they are good. He knows that they just need to think, like Roux told him once. They need to think and learn that it is important to wait for your second thought, and not just think your first. That flowers can turn to fruit, if you let them. That there are stories about animals changing and plants growing and hungry caterpillars becoming butterflies if they eat the right sort of thing. Malkin knows he just has to find a way of explaining that to his friends, and, if he can, they might let peace in.

And he knows immediately and at once what he has to do.

As the other cats walk away discussing the news, Roux winds herself close to Malkin.

'I know why I'm here, Roux.'

'Yes,' she says. 'So do I.'

'Those poor cats. Their home will be flattened. Diggers will come and take away all the rubbish. Great big diggers that could run over a cat and not even know.'

'Malkin?'

'Yes, Roux?'

'If anyone can find a way it's you. We've *always* known you have a destiny to help others. The moon knows it too – I read it in your sixth sense all that time ago, the day after you fell off the seawall.'

'Thank you, Roux.'

She pushes her nose against his. 'If there is a way, you will find it.' Then she smiles, and raises her smoke and cream tail, and leaves Malkin to think.

Chapter 34

Home

'Toxic is my friend. He won't hurt me,' Malkin says to Roux the following night.

'I know that you have been helping him, but still I'm not sure,' says Roux. 'I don't like the idea of you going over there. Let me tell the others so they can be ready in case you need us. We can watch from the wall. Oh, I don't want to lose you, Malkin.'

'You're not going to lose me, Roux,' Malkin says, 'I promise. You know this is what I was destined to do.'

'I *do* know that, Malkin, but it does not make me less afraid. Can I come with you?'

'No. If there were two of us they might not trust us. This is something I have to do alone. Please don't worry.'

Malkin jumps over the wall and sets off down Cats' Alley, treading softly. But immediately Calica bounces up to him, a ball of moonlit white.

'Oh my! I've been waiting to see you,' she cries. 'I knew you'd come! Thank you for saving me. I've wanted to say thank you for a really long time, and Daddy said it's you who puts the food by the wall for us and makes the calling sound when it is safe to come over to eat.'

'Yes, that is me, and I'm glad because you've grown so much, Calica!'

'I know! I am barely even a kitten now.'

'How are you? How is your tail?'

Calica does a little spin, 'Look, it mended completely. I'm really excited you've come to visit. I've asked Mummy and Daddy a hundred times if you could come.'

Malkin's sixth sense prickles and he sees Salt approaching him cautiously.

'Oh, Mummy, can we take Malkin to see our home? It's a very beautiful home.'

Salt looks at her kitten and nose-bumps her. 'Thank you, my darling, but the home is just for our kind.'

'But Malkin *is* our kind, Mummy. Look! He's a cat.'

Malkin looks at Salt. 'I would be honoured to visit your home.'

'Very well,' she says. 'It's this way.'

They turn and follow Cats' Alley all the way to the Putrescibles' home.

It is a collection of broken crates and plastic bowls and scratched-out containers all stacked against each other in a ramshackle fashion. There are butts set out to collect rainwater, but the water inside them looks dirty.

'In here,' says Salt, and pushes open a curtain that has been draped across a large crate.

It is completely dark. From within, eight shining retinas meet Malkin's eyes. The voices that come out are hisses. It smells of night-time, and the corners of secret spaces where the spiders live, and sweetness, all at the same time – like Foss smelled when he had the terrible fever. For a moment Malkin remembers his cellar in the pub, and his heart fills up with the thought of Roux.

'What in the name of the moon are you doing, Salt, bringing him in here?' Phobos asks, appearing in the doorway. It is clear he is struggling to keep his claws inside his paws.

'The black cat should not be here,' says the delicate voice of Orchid from within.

'I wanted to see where you live. I want you to know I have respect for you,' Malkin replies.

'He is welcome here,' says Toxic, walking out of the shadows to stand by Phobos. 'He is the cat who leaves the food out for us.'

Toxic looks at Malkin, and his face is kind. He doesn't say the word friend, but it is in the air all around them.

'Come inside, Malkin. See how beautiful it is!' says Calica, jumping up on her tippy-toes.

Malkin steps inside and looks around. Immediately his heart sinks with sorrow. 'Yes, Calica, it's a very beautiful home; it is full of love.'

Then he has to turn to hide his face. He pretends he is studying the old, dirty piece of carpet that is draped across the ceiling to keep the rain out. But really he has to hide how angry he is feeling.

The worst sort of anger: he is angry with himself.

He has not done enough. He has been living happily on his side of the wall, while over here these cats are living in squalor and suffering hunger.

'I knew you'd like it,' Calica says, bouncing up and down on all fours. 'There is so much to smell here and taste, but you must be careful. You mustn't drink the water on the ground and you must be careful where you put your paws. But you can play the game of keeping away from the methane gas that spurts up out of the ground sometimes. It's fun: you never know when it's going to happen!'

'Toxic and Salt, I must talk to you,' Malkin says. 'Please. Is there a place we can go that is private?'

The two cats look at each other. Then Salt speaks. 'Yes, there is an old bath that we have our meetings in. It is safe to sit in as the bad stuff leaks out through the plug-hole. It's this way.'

Malkin follows the two cats through the darkness to the bathtub. They settle in it and fold their tails neatly.

'I have come to tell you something,' Malkin begins.

'Go on,' says Toxic.

'It is bad news, I'm afraid. This side of the wall – your home – is to become a nature park.'

Toxic and Salt look at each other. 'What does that mean, Malkin?' Toxic asks.

'It means that soon diggers will come and take away all the waste. Your home will be taken away. It will be a very dangerous time.'

Salt lets out a cry and buries her face in her husband's neck. 'Oh! Oh, what can we do? We will have to move, Toxic. We will have to make a long, dangerous journey to find a new home.'

'When will this happen?' Toxic asks.

'I think soon,' says Malkin, and he raises his nose to the inky sky and looks for the moon, but she is hiding behind clouds tonight and does not sail out to help him, 'but I don't know exactly. We read it in the newspaper, but it didn't say when.'

'So it could be any day?' Toxic says.

'That is what I am afraid of,' Malkin replies, 'so we have very little time. There is no option now: we must create peace among us.'

'But how?' Salt asks, and her voice is full of worry.

214

'I have an idea,' says Malkin, 'but I will need the very thing that is the most precious to you.'

Salt flashes her eyes at Malkin. 'No,' she says.

'Yes,' says Malkin. 'I will need to borrow Calica.'

Chapter 35

Peace

The moon is almost full the night that Malkin calls his friends for a meeting. He sits upon the wall.

The cats sit in front of him, their tails wrapped tightly, their eyes aglow.

The moon watches from behind.

Below the wall, on the other side, Malkin can feel the anxious presence of two other cats, and the excitement of one.

'My friends …' Malkin says, and he looks down at the blue one, the white one, the silver-grey one, and the tiger-striped one. Then he looks aside at the one he loves, and she smiles, and he sees her faith in him.

'I would like you to meet a friend of mine. This is Calica.'

There is a scampering sound, and up on the wall appears Calica. She has crowned herself in all the flowers and berries she could find for this special night.

'Malkin!' shrieks Marmelade. 'Be careful! That's a Putrescible.'

'Oh my,' says Calica, and she is so sad that her head falls forward and her crown falls off.

'Marmelade,' says Malkin, 'Calica is not a Putrescible.'

'What on earth do you mean, Malkin? She *is* a Putrescible, as certain as I am a pure-blooded Chartreux. Her mother is Salt and her father is Toxic. She is Putrescible through and through.' Marmelade looks around for support. 'Isn't she, Foss?'

But Foss is amazed at how the little kitten he helped save has grown. He is wondering if Sonata ever had a kitten whether she would be as beautiful as the one sitting bravely on the wall. Would she glow as white? Would her face be as pretty? And deep down he knows she would be. Foss imagines that he can almost see the kitten, here, in the moonlight in front of him … so he hardly hears Marmelade's words and he definitely forgets to answer.

'Marmelade,' Malkin's voice is quite cross, 'this is Calica. She is a kitten, the same as you were, the same as I was.'

And Roux remembers when Malkin was barely more than a kitten, and was hungry, just like the kitten on the wall. And Roux knows that Malkin *will* do this, he will convince his friends, because he is Malkin Moonlight, and he is a special cat, steered by kindness and enabled by bravery and gifted by the moon.

But for now she knows the way she can help. So Roux pads up to the wall and looks up and speaks gently. 'Calica, would you like to come down here with me? You know, I quite forgot to have supper tonight and I'd *really* love a midnight feast.'

'Yes, please! That sounds so exciting.' Calica jumps down and Roux picks up her crown of flowers in her mouth and places it back on her head. Then Calica follows Roux into the shadows between the bins.

Malkin waits until they are out of sight.

'My friends. Any day now – we don't know when – the diggers will come and take away the waste, then flatten the land on the other side of this wall.'

'Good,' says Marmelade. 'There is a terrible smell tonight. It is very strong.'

'And what sort of cats would we be if we sat here in comfort, knowing our own kind are in extreme danger? Our side has expanded. There is plenty of room for everyone and there is even more food in the new lorries. The men in gloves are kind to us. Why can't we make peace? Why can't we invite the other cats to live on this side too?'

'Because of the war that has always been,' says Marmelade. 'It is the history of this place. It is a lot like the history of France.'

'But don't we think it's time for it to stop? No one can even remember why it started. Do we want to be the generation of cats who let the war continue until the other side was destroyed? Or do you want to be remembered by your kittens as the generation of cats who brought peace?'

'But what about Sage?' asks Marmelade. 'He was our friend. Toxic killed him.'

'That was an accident, Marmelade,' Dew says, from the shadows. 'Toxic has explained. Malkin, please continue.'

'In order for peace to work, we have to learn to say sorry. We have to forget the bad things we have done, or that others have done to us, so that we can become happier, with more friends and an even better community.'

'But it is so hard to forget,' says Marmelade.

'But can you try, Marmelade? Can you try for us all?' Malkin asks. 'Because if we can create peace, we all win.'

'I am thinking about it,' says Marmelade. 'Give me the time to think.'

'I vote for peace,' says Dew. 'I have one life left, and it would be the greatest happiness of my final life to know that war is over, and that kittens will grow on this side of the wall, and Roux and Malkin will teach them to read, and our Recycling Centre home will have a happy future.'

'Foss?' Sonata asks quietly.

'Peace,' he says.

'Are you sure?'

He puts a paw on her paw. 'I am, I really am. For my ancestors. Malkin is right; these are my relatives. Once we were all one family. We can be again. A family.' And he smiles at the beautiful face of Sonata, and she smiles back.

Just then the shapes of Roux and Calica appear out of the shadows.

'Thank you,' Calica is saying. 'That was the most delicious thing I have ever tasted. You are so kind. Just wait till I tell Mummy how it tasted. We have never had anything like that on our side.'

Foss whispers to Sonata, 'She's white, just like you.'

'She's lovely,' Sonata replies, 'and she's related to you.'

Which is the exact moment when Foss dares to think

something else, although he doesn't have the courage to say it, not just yet, but he will.

'Calica, you are always welcome over here for food,' says Sonata in her gentle voice.

'Oh, thank you. You remind me of my mummy. But I wish that the other cats could come too.'

Marmelade rolls her copper-coloured eyes at the sky. 'Oh, Malkin, I give in. What is the point? Look at the face of Foss. He is enchanted. Sonata too. You win. The war is over. Let the Putrescibles come over; they can live on this side.'

'Oh!' cries Calica, jumping up on her tippy-toes. 'Do you mean it, beautiful blue lady cat?'

'You have very good eyesight,' says Marmelade, 'and I do mean it. I always mean what I say.'

'Oh, thank you.'

'So, cats, please raise your paws if you are in agreement,' Malkin says.

And all the cats sit on three paws and raise one.

'Good. From this day on, let there not be Putrescible, Domestic or Wild; we are all cat-kind. We look after each other. There are many dangerous things around us, but if we can take care of each other we will all be stronger. We all live under the same moon.'

'Truly?' asks Calica, looking at the other cats.

'Truly,' says Sonata.

'Of course,' says Dew, and he sounds happy.

'*Oui*,' says Marmelade.

Foss nods. 'Yes,' he says, 'it is time to forgive.' And he looks at Toxic, and he smiles.

'Goodbye, everyone,' says Calica, raising a white paw. 'See you soon.'

'Goodbye, Calica,' call the cats.

And Malkin and Calica jump over the wall and land next to an anxious Toxic and Salt, who have been listening to every word.

'You have done it,' says Toxic.

'Thank you,' says Salt, holding her kitten tight.

But Malkin does not need thanks. He looks up to the moon and feels her pride in him running inside his blood and his sinews.

'Peace,' he says. 'So this is how it feels.'

And he thinks it might be his favourite feeling of all.

'I loved this night,' Malkin whispers to Roux later in Mattresses.

She stretches out a paw for his. 'I know, Malkin.

This was the night you were perfectly yourself. This was the night you were made for. I am *extremely* proud of you.'

'Thank you, Roux. I am so proud of you too. This feels wonderful,' he says. 'The other cats are going to gather up their few precious things and come over the wall tomorrow. Then we will be united.'

'Oh, Malkin. You have done what the moon wanted so *perfectly*.'

'I hope I have. Goodnight, Roux.'

'Goodnight, Malkin.'

Chapter 36
Horatio Lands

It is perhaps because the cats stayed up so late that they are still asleep early the following morning when Horatio lands in Mattresses with a squawk.

'Cat friends, I have come to warn you: a great army of diggers has arrived on the other side of the wall. They are progressing up Cats' Alley.'

As one the cats sit up and lift their ears and hear the noise of the engines, but Malkin is already on his feet. 'Then I must go and help our friends.'

'Malkin,' shouts Roux, 'you *mustn't*! It's too dangerous.'

But Malkin is already gone.

The first thing he sees from the top of the wall is a tall orange digger, with a long neck and a great big extending claw that eats into the ground with its teeth and lifts waste high, then twists around and drops its load into a trailer. Behind that a big lorry that says 'MAN' on it is coming down Cats' Alley, while two yellow diggers are going forwards and backwards across it, beeping angrily and ripping at the rubbish with their sharp claws, then throwing it high with their long necks. The yellow diggers have big grilles in front of them that they push through the waste and huge spiky wheels that squash everything in their path.

An angry orange digger turns and comes towards the wall with its enormous mouth open, its neck craning towards Malkin, all its teeth sharp …

… and Malkin leaps towards it

and

lands

in danger.

Everywhere the stench is stronger than ever as the diggers churn up the waste. The noises all around are so loud that it is difficult to use his senses, but Malkin does not turn off hearing, as a backwards digger makes a beeping sound and a forwards digger makes a primeval, guttural roar. Malkin knows he needs to hear the noises to help him stay safe.

Half of Cats' Alley is gone. Scooped up and tipped away. Everywhere is the sound of beeping and roaring and he has to be careful not to be crushed beneath the enormous tyres.

Malkin thinks of his friends – where are they? Did they run at the first noise? Are they sheltered somewhere? Or is it already too late? Close up, the wheels of the diggers look even more enormous: the huge, spiky tyres can even climb. Everything in their way is lifted or squashed, lifted or squashed.

He must focus. He must use his sixth to find his friends, and, once he has, he must guide them safely back across the wall. That is his job. That is what the moon meant. His sixth is strong, stronger than ever; it can pull him in the right direction and it can lead him and the others back, the safest way, avoiding danger.

But everything here is too stinky and too loud and too confusing.

The glass beneath his paws is sharp. Thousands of broken pieces shine everywhere. The poison that leaks and burns is everywhere. Even the air is full of tiny, dangerous things that tickle now, and make him sneeze, but Malkin knows that later they will hurt and sting and make his eyes cry.

All around is bad.

Ahead a lorry starts moving towards him. It is the big lorry with 'MAN' written on the front.

But Malkin closes his eyes.

He stands still amid all the chaos.

He knows that behind him Roux will be calling his name from the top of the wall. He knows that in front of him his friends may be trapped or worse. He wishes it was night-time so the moon could gently illuminate his path – but there is no time to wait for that. Any moment now one of those enormous claws could rip a cat from the earth, lift it high and bury it under a tonne of rubble.

Or those enormous tyres could run over a cat and not even feel it. Not know that it had taken all the lives of an animal and left it there, dead. Up ahead he sees the horror of twisted wire blocking his path.

He pushes his nose under it, wriggles low, and comes out the other side.

He listens carefully for the pull of his sixth sense, but all around is too noisy and smelly and confusing.

And now Malkin knows he has no choice.

He turns off all his senses but his sixth.

And he runs with that.

Malkin races down what is left of Cats' Alley. Even though the way is no longer clear, and all around is starting to look the same, Malkin can sense that this is the pathway – that many cats have walked up and down it over the years since 2001. The first part of the pathway is gone now – cleared, but not clean. Everything that contained liquid has been lifted and has spilt its contents, everything that was smashed has dropped its sharp pieces, and some things have fallen clear: squashed footballs and old boots and shoes.

Malkin's paws run through it all. He runs until he feels the alley is there again, and so he turns his sight back on.

And at the end he can see the cats' ramshackle home. It looks small and vulnerable and so easy, so very easy, to destroy.

Malkin runs. And as he runs he turns on his hearing, and he hears the fast approach of a digger behind him. The very digger that is eating up Cats' Alley. He must outrun it before its teeth can bite and lift up the home. Malkin thinks of Calica, bouncing on her tippy-toes, saying what a beautiful home they had. It is full of love, Malkin remembers saying, and it was true.

But just as he reaches the plastic water butts an enormous claw leans over Malkin and rips away the ground in front of him. Malkin just manages to bat aside the carpet to look inside.

It is empty.

They are not there.

They have got away.

He is filled with huge relief. *Not here*, he thinks, *so where?*

He turns to look behind him, just as the huge claw comes back down, scoops Malkin from the ground, whizzes him round and throws him.

Chapter 37

Five Lives

When Malkin wakes up all is still and it is the half-light that cats like best. He shakes himself. He is covered in dirt and dust. He checks his tail, his paws, his eyes, his ears. Nothing is lost, nothing is broken, but something has changed.

Two more lives have gone.

Two at once.

He thinks of Roux. Two fewer lives to live with her. Now he is a cat with just five lives to her eight. It doesn't feel like enough.

Poor Roux. She will be so worried.

His head aches and it feels sharp behind his eyes so he ruffles up the white fur around his neck and he speaks quietly to himself.

'I am Malkin Moonlight,' he says, out loud for comfort, 'and I can do this. If my friends are still alive, I will find them and I will rescue them, and then the two lives I have lost will not matter, because I will have saved many lives. It is as the moon would want.'

Malkin stretches out a paw, not sure what he will touch. He pushes and then there is the milky calm of moonlight. He pushes and leaps and then he stands and surveys the scene. He had been buried beneath the dirt.

He shakes his fur and he sneezes.

A cat with five lives.

Five, he thinks. *Five*.

Then he considers that a cat can do a lot with five lives, and he walks on.

All around him is the insistent sound of explosion. Bang after bang after bang troubling the sky, troubling his senses.

He looks up, and in the black distance he sees gold appear, and flicker as if it is alive, and fall happily like water, and vanish. Then something red shoots into the highest part of the sky, where it exists for a beautiful moment, then dies, and the sky turns to black as if it never happened. A second later the sky's memory changes and now it is filled with a shot of green, sharp green, like Malkin's own eyes, which lives for a brilliant moment.

More lights flare up and are one colour, and then become another, and they spin in whirls as if they are chasing their tails in almighty circles.

'Oh!' says Malkin, watching the sky for more, because the sky is beautiful, even if the sounds are fearful and make his tail rise and his fur prickle.

He pushes his ears back and moves on, but his paws keep jumping because he hates the bangs so, and there is a smell of heat and fire in the air and the smell of the rubbish that has been turned over after so long revealing the dark secrets of what was lying underneath. Malkin turns his ears to the music of the stars, the eternal song that plays even when all around is desolate. But the noises are so loud, too loud, so he turns off his sense of hearing and listens only to his heart and his sixth sense.

They were not in Cats' Alley, he thinks, and I am glad of that, but where can they be? And he listens inside for the pull of his sixth sense, and the pull of his heart, because he knows instinct and love will help him find his friends.

Eyes closed, ears closed, paws lifted, whiskers trembling, Malkin walks slowly, slowly, silent and black, holding his stomach tightly above the rotten earth, carefully, carefully picking up his paws and following the faint pull, that is just something, just there, the tiniest tickle of a feeling, like the very end of a whisker against your face, and perhaps he is imagining it, and his head does hurt, but no, it is true, there is a feeling. Black paw over black paw, not thinking of what he is treading on, Malkin follows the pull, until it grows thicker, and stronger, from a whisker into a piece of string, and then fatter still, more like rope, and he thinks of the boats harboured in the sea and how they tugged and how he first ran with Roux, and how he has lost two lives without her, and how badly his head is hurting, how bad it is that perhaps he is going to lose another, but no, focus, Malkin, keep going.

And the tug gets stronger and stronger until …

Malkin stops.

He turns back on all his senses.

He is at the edge of a big pit.

At the bottom is a bath, half buried in the rubbish, and coming out from under it is a long, stripy tail. 'Toxic!' Malkin shouts. 'Toxic! I have found you. Don't worry, it's me, Malkin. I'm coming.'

And he raises his great black tail and half runs, half jumps, down the side of the pit as the stars stutter against the tremors of the noisy colours in their night sky.

Malkin lands on the bath. He knows he cannot lift it, so his only hope is that the buried part of it is broken, or lying at an angle. He starts to dig.

He digs and digs until he uncovers a jagged hole where the bath has been dropped and smashed. And through the hole Malkin can see the shining of his friends' eyes. They blink up at him.

They are alive.

But …

Malkin goes faster, pulling away the final rubbish that is blocking the entrance. Then he reaches out a paw and pulls out Salt, Calica, Orchid, Yellow and Toxic through the space he has created.

Then Malkin reaches one final time into the darkness and he finds a paw, and Toxic helps him pull, but what they all suspect, in the sixth senses inside them, is true after all.

Phobos is unmoving. His amber eyes stare up, towards where the digger had struck him.

All the cats cry.

The wind wails.

The night waits.

The stars call silent sounds across the blackness to comfort each other.

'They've all gone,' says Salt softly, 'all his lives at once. It is no good. We have to leave brave Phobos to the long, quiet sleep.'

'He will always be a young cat, in his prime,' says Malkin, and he turns and looks for something, anything beautiful in this cursed place to mark where Phobos fell.

But there is nothing, so Malkin lifts his face to the moon.

'Please, oh Moon.'

And he need say no more than that. The moon rises and shines her luminescence on the body of Phobos.

All the cats hear her words at once, inside them and outside them and dancing all around.

'I will stay with him while he makes the longest journey, and carry him through the great fall between dreams and up into the huge rise,' she says. 'Death does not last. Go now, little cats. This is not your time. You have further to go and more lives to live.'

'Thank you, oh Moon,' says Malkin with a bow.

Then the cats turn away, and they leave their friend,

and together they walk towards the great wall that has divided their kind.

Then, with an easy spring and tails held high, six cats scale it.

And a moment later they all land on the same side.

Chapter 38

Colour

'Pardon me for saying it,' begins Yellow the following morning, when all the cats are eating breakfast, 'but your eyes are the most beautiful I've ever seen. And I know why you're called Marmalade, now I'm eating it for the first time. Look –' he holds up a sticky paw – 'it's because your eyes are the exact same colour and they've got the sharpness of its taste and they're deep like it too.'

Marmelade stops eating her breakfast. For a moment she is silent. Then she finds her voice.

'I beg your pardon?' she asks quietly.

The yellow cat opens his eyes wide, but patiently explains again.

All the while he is talking, the yellow cat keeps eating, but his words are so wonderful Marmelade finds herself not caring too much about his manners.

Eventually she shakes out her blue double-fur coat and lifts her glorious eyes once more to his.

'Monsieur,' she begins, 'are you saying you can see in colour?'

'It's strange, I know,' Yellow says, moving on to a tiny jar of anchovies. 'Bother, can't get my paw in this one. I'll have to smash it.'

'Do not smash it, you will make the most terrible mess. We tip those ones, like this, see?'

'Oh yes, Marmalade. How clever you are. Thanking you kindly. Oh, delicious. We didn't get grub like this over on the other side. We often went for days with barely anything. Hard it was, stomach can't get used to such fine food. Sure it will though, my lady.'

'*Oui*, but now you will be living on this side. And so you were speaking about my eyes. You can see their precise shade? Is this true, what you are saying?'

'Oh yes, Marmalade. When I first saw you I didn't think you were real. I said to the others, I said, "A blue cat!" Who knew? Thought I was seeing things, truth be told. But you're real all right. And you smell something marvellous. And your coat is a wonderful colour, but the real thing about you is your eyes. They're like when the sun is lowest in the sky. Or the copper pipes that get chucked on the other side. Or the marmalade you're eating now. They are really the most terrific colour.'

'*Mon Dieu*, I cannot believe it. You *can* see in colour.'

'Yes, my lady, I can. It's true.'

'It's true, but that is not what I mean – I mean it is incredible. It is a gift, *chéri*, a gift.'

'Nah – no one has ever said I have a gift. They all call me stupid.'

'You? Stupid? *Non*, you are not stupid. I think that you are the most clever of cats, because you can appreciate what truly matters. And what truly matters is beauty.'

'It is a joy forever, Marmalade.'

'Now that is four times. Let us get this right if we are to go any further. It is Marme*lade*. The French way. Not the English. You do not say the *e* at the end. You swallow the *e*.'

'I beg your pardon, Marme*lade*,' says Yellow, gulping the e at the end.

'Just so. Now the thing about my eyes, could you say it again? Exactly the same.'

'Didn't you hear it the first time?'

'My ears are very good, I assure you. I am a Chartreux and we have very fine hearing. It is just a long, long time since anyone appreciated the colour of my eyes. Not since my Owner died.'

'I'm sorry to hear that. Of course I can tell you about your eyes.'

'And then perhaps you could talk a little more about the colour of my coat.'

'Not a problem. I could talk about the colour of your coat practically forever.'

'Then perhaps we can stroll to my armoire. I have kept a few treats in there that I would like to share with a friend.'

'A friend?'

'*Oui*.'

'Well, then, yes, of course I can tell you about your colours. Let me see. Look at me and I'll do my best. Your eyes …'

'What is that sound?' asks Sonata. 'It's a very beautiful sound.'

'Oh, that's Mummy singing,' says Calica, licking her paw. 'She sings all the time.'

'Oh,' says Sonata, 'does she really?'

'Yes, she's very musical. It's her dearest wish to form a choir.'

'A choir?'

'Yes, a cat choir, but no one else on our old side could sing very well. Can you sing, Sonata?'

'Oh yes, Calica! Singing is quite my favourite thing because I used to be a cathedral cat. I grew up with music around me. Foss is good at singing too, although he won't admit it, but I've caught him on many evenings lately, humming up at the moon.'

'Here comes Daddy now,' says Calica. 'He's great at whistling – Daddy and Yellow like to whistle tunes together. They did it all the time on the other side to keep us happy. And Orchid is good with blowing in bottles. Do you know you can make different notes if you fill bottles up with water?'

'Yes, I do know that! I'll go and find Foss now and we can start our cat choir and orchestra. Dew has some sheet music in his library so he can be the conductor. How exciting! Do stay here, Calica, while I fetch Foss and Dew.'

'And Malkin and Roux,' says Calica. 'I don't want to sing without them. Let's all join in together. All of us.'

'Yes,' says Sonata, pausing to smile at the kitten, 'all together. That will be just perfect.'

Chapter 39

Long-Night Moon

It is a very special night, under the light of the long-night moon, when the cats gather by Entrance/Exit and raise their noses to the roof of the new expansion, where Sonata and Foss are talking to the moon in private.

The moon hangs low in the sky, vast and cold. White, delicate flakes land on the cats' noses.

'Oh, Malkin, do you remember?' asks Roux.

'Of course I do,' says Malkin. 'It was the happiest night of my life.'

'I *knew* you had something special to do, Malkin, and you've done it. Look around you. Look how happy everyone is.'

'But I couldn't have done it without you by my side, nor without all the things you have taught me and all the faith you have had in me, even when I doubted myself. Especially then.'

'I have *loved* the things we have done together. You have taught me life, Malkin. This *is* life, and I am so proud of you.'

'As I am of you.'

'This feeling now, Malkin, right now, this is as happy as I can be. Oh, but don't we feel grown-up, suddenly? It seems like yesterday that we were kittens, and I didn't feel the changes happening, but now I look at us and realise that we are grown. How did that happen? How is it you blink and things are different?'

'Some things don't change, Roux,' Malkin says, looking into her eyes. The long-night moon behind their ears creates their silhouettes: an *MM* against her vast white circle, with two question-mark tails raised high. Then Malkin smiles, and both cats raise their faces to the starry night.

'Look, Malkin,' says Roux. 'They have put their paws against their hearts.'

'And now they are kneeling down! Ah, look, they are closing their eyes. Now they will have the wonderful feeling that the moon gives them.'

Then the moon rises, and all the cats, both high up and low down, are bathed in the luminescence of her light, and they watch the silhouette of Foss stand and hold out his paw to the silhouette of Sonata.

243

'Oh, I must go up to the roof, Malkin. Salt and I have rehearsed a song for their wedding dance.'

And in a whisk of cream and smoke Roux is away, and a few moments later she appears with Salt on the roof of the new expansion, where they raise their noses to the long-night moon and sing a song so beautiful that even the stars join in. Then, as one, the animals head to the broken floodlights that flash off and on where a feast has been laid out.

Yellow and Marmelade sit to share the remains of a pot of Gentleman's Relish. Yellow passes Marmelade a Large Salmon and Tuna Box from the sushi restaurant.

'Thank you, Yellow. You are *très gentil.*'

'There's some salad and avocado in that one you'll want to pick out, but the rest is delicious.'

'I'll just take a little; perhaps just the sashimi,' says Marmelade, scooping three fat pieces of salmon on her claws and pushing the box along to Dew. 'I cannot believe it, it is only two days past its sell-by. Humans are so particular. Ah, here comes my friend Horatio. There is plenty for everyone, Horatio, although I am surprised to see you up so late.'

'Ahoy there, shipmates!' says Horatio, landing and folding his wings neatly. 'My what a spread. Yes,

Marmelade, usually I would be abed by now, but I didn't want to miss the feast. May I?'

'But, *chéri*, you must help yourself to your heart's content. This is my new friend Yellow – I don't believe you've met. Yellow, this is Horatio.'

'Hello, old chap.'

'Pleased to meet you, mate.'

'Yellow can see in colour, Horatio. Can you believe this news? He can see the *exact* shade of my fur and the *precise* colour of my eyes. He is *very* civilised. *Très*, as we say in France.'

Sonata dabs inside a glass pot that contains ten balls of caviar.

'Happy?' Foss asks.

'Very,' says Sonata, and she touches his nose again, softly, because she is allowed to now, all the time, so she thinks that she always will.

Foss closes his eye, and Sonata stares at the face she loves best in the world, and hopes to always, always bring him happiness.

Calica runs around sniffing and exploring everything, her little paws in all the different kinds of food.

She runs up to Malkin and Roux. 'Oh my, it's so exciting here: everything is so beautiful tonight.

I cannot believe the moon is so big. And Mummy and Daddy say I can stay up as late as I like, for one night only, because it is a special night, for Sonata and Foss.'

'It is a *very* special night,' agrees Roux.

'But I do wish there were other kittens to explore with. Then life would be just wonderful. Oh! There's

Marmelade, I must talk to her, she's teaching me French, I love learning, it's so interesting. Goodbye!'

As Malkin and Roux watch Calica run off, their paws find each other, and then their cold noses, and they rub into the soft fur around each other's necks. Then Malkin lifts his paw, and Roux offers hers, and they dance under the light of the long-night moon.

Chapter 40
Big News

It was time for the news. All the cats sat and waited nicely.

'Today I have some news that is for Roux,' says Dew.

'Oh,' says Roux, her ears pricking up. 'Big news or little news?'

'For you I think it is big news.'

'I am brave,' says Roux, for she detects a quiver in Dew's voice, as if he is afraid to hurt her feelings. 'You can show us all. I have no secrets from my friends.'

'Very well, here it is.' Dew holds up the newspaper. 'I think I am right – this is your Owner?' It is a double-page spread and there are two photographs. Roux lets out a mew, and Malkin leans into her.

'It is,' she says in her softest voice.

'Poor *chérie*. It is her Owner.'

There is a photograph of La Chatte Grise restaurant.

Next to it is writing about the chef and Cecilia. Cecilia is sitting at a table and on the table Roux sees her old basket. In the basket is a cream-and-smoke-coloured cat.

'My sister!' says Roux. 'That is my sister grown big! The chef must have let my Owner go back to the white house I was born in – and this time she chose my sister! Oh, this *is* big news, this is big news indeed!'

Malkin touches her paw, right where the star is. 'Your Owner looks very happy.'

'She is, and that makes *me* happy. Can I keep the photograph, Dew?'

'It is yours.'

'I will stick it to my mattress. So I can always see my Owner. She will always be there, she will always be an Owner to me. Malkin?' asks Roux quietly then, with a gentle touch of her paw.

'Yes, Roux?'

'There's one more thing. I have some news too.'

'What is it?'

'Can we go somewhere private? There's something I need to tell you ...'

'Of course, but what is it?'

A moment later Malkin nuzzles into Roux's neck. 'How many?' he asks softly.

Roux smiles, 'I *think* two. I think I can feel eight paws. Two kittens, Malkin. We are to have two kittens.'

'Oh, Roux. I do love you.'

'And I love you, Malkin. I love you *very* much.'

Epilogue

'Look at them playing, Malkin, our little moon kittens.'

'Mimosa's just like you – she's so fast. Look how quick her reactions are: she'd be a good fighter, if there was any fighting left to do. Look how she loves exploring – just like you did, Roux; as soon as I persuaded you over the seawall there was no stopping you.'

'Marmelade told me this morning that she is setting up a play area in Small Domestic Items. Just some hoops and tunnels and safe places to explore, some high-up fun, some balancing areas. Oh, and she's found a coatstand made out of metal coat hangers at all different angles: there is lots of slipping and sliding to be had. Dew's collecting books for a children's library. He's found my favourite book about a caterpillar, and a different one about a rat with no name, and one about an owl who is afraid, and several about Domestics, and one all about

Wild Things. It will be *very* educational for them; I can't *wait* to teach all the new kittens to read. Calica loves reading – goodness, she must be the age that you were when you started to learn with me in the pub. Do you remember, Malkin?'

'How could I forget?'

Without thought, their tail tips meet and twine behind them.

'I'm going to meet Yellow over in Fridges and Freezers. He wants my advice about something. He says it's private.'

'You go, Malkin. I'm going to sit up here and watch the kittens play. It was *so* kind of the moon to bless Crispin and Mimosa with white socks to keep their paws safe on their wanderings – you can just *tell* they're brother and sister. And she put a tiny full moon on Mimosa's forehead ...' For a moment both cats fall silent and share thoughts, for the moon has said that Mimosa is going to be special, that she has something rare inside her, but her parents are not to tell her. She said that Mimosa's heart may pull her away one day when she is older, and that Malkin and Roux are not to stop her.

'Mimosa will be a fine explorer with good deeds to do for cat-kind and for all. You must let her go, when the time comes, when her sixth sense and her heart pull her away.

I have given her my blessing in the full moon on her forehead and the two white socks on her front paws. She will step lightly into trouble, and spring lightly away.'

'But will she come back?' Roux had asked. 'Will she come home to our Recycling Centre?'

'Ah, that knowledge is written in the stars,' the moon answered. 'Only the stars know and they do not tell, they just tingle. Crispin is clever and strong. I have blessed his back paws. While Mimosa is a leader, he is a leaper. Time and tide will tell what he is to be.'

'Oh, Malkin,' says Roux, and a new sound escapes her – like a chirrup – because she has got a whole new sense, and that is motherhood, and the pull of it is the strongest pull she has ever felt.

'I know,' Malkin says. 'Oh, Roux, I know.'

Both cats think about their kittens, and Roux rubs her neck into the white hoop around Malkin's neck. Somehow it always makes her feel better. Then she looks back down.

'Oh, look who's coming! I *love* that Plato has Sonata's white fur but Foss's black stripes. Look at the way he walks! He's so sweet – he lifts his feet up high like he's dancing and keeps his nose pointed to the sky. I've never seen a kitten step more lightly. He looks so happy with his face up like that.'

Roux places her paw on Malkin's and they look at the star the moon gave her.

Then Malkin looks up at the sun. 'It's time,' he says. 'I'd better go to meet Yellow, see how I can help him.'

Roux and Malkin touch noses, and for a moment they blink and their ears move forward. Then Roux wraps her tail around herself and sits up on the box. She looks down at her moon kittens playing, then jumps a few boxes closer and hides herself, hoping that their sixth senses aren't strong enough yet to feel her, so she can watch – just to check they don't get themselves in trouble and that Mimosa doesn't go over the wall to where the men in gloves are planting the trees.

But Mimosa has promised not to, so she *ought* to trust her really, it's just that she's *so* like her father and Crispin is no better: gravity has such a slim grip on him.

Malkin walks through the Recycling Centre, his great tail held high. He looks up to where the waxing crescent moon is just visible. She is never strong in the daytime, but sometimes she can be seen, and today is one of those days. Malkin jumps on top of a green bin. He bows his head and presses his nose into the cold metal. He feels a *whoosh* as the tail end of a gust of cold north wind flicks over him and ruffles the white ring around his neck.

'Oh Moon,' he begins, 'I need to thank you. I have Roux, and my moon kittens, and we are so happy. I have tried my best always to be kind. I have found a home, and for now the pull inside me is quite, quite gone. In fact, it is keeping me here. This is a place full of love and happiness and friendship. Thank you for your wisdom, oh Moon. You have guided me well, and I hope that one day you will guide Crispin and Mimosa.'

The daytime moon is not strong enough to send a reply, but she soaks up Malkin's words, and they make her quite full of pride for the little black cat with the big tail that she named all that time ago.

'And I have learned the power of peace, Moon, and that you need it for love to grow. And I understand about love. I learned about that all by myself. It is something that cannot be taught, it can only be felt, and it grows bigger and bigger and more and more. Once you start loving it is difficult to stop.'

Then Malkin Moonlight looks up for a moment and blinks. 'And I am glad about that.'

He bows once more, and then he jumps from the bin. He knows there will be other threats, other things that could pull him away, but now, right now, Malkin feels happy.

He feels as happy as a cat can be.

And cats can be *very* happy.

Acknowledgements

I feel very, very lucky that this book has been published, so I would like to thank some people who are important in my life, and who, in one way or another, have helped me become an author.

I wrote *Malkin Moonlight* because my best friend, Katherine Andrews, has the faith in me that I often lack myself. Thank you, Strega. I cannot conceive of a more beautiful or loyal friend. Here's to having A Time and going on Club Med holidays during tropical storms, and dancing to Guetta and snorkelling and talking to pelicans.

I love children's books because of my mother, so this book is for her. As she reminds me, I have wanted to be an author since I was three years old. That's because she engendered a love of reading in me from when I was tiny. Half my creativity comes from my father, and I love him so dearly; he is the best father in the world. I have relied on my parents' love my whole life and I am grateful for the happiness they have given me and their absolute faith in me. Thanks too to my lovely brother Harry, my beautiful sister Hermione and my amazing niece Cecilia, who loves seagulls and whose voice I have borrowed in this book. 'This is life!' comes straight from her. I love you with all my heart.

Jonathan Douglas of the National Literacy Trust. It was so lovely to hear you read my words on stage. And so surprising. You brought them to life and I couldn't believe they were my own. Thank you for this opportunity, and thank you for being so funny, charismatic and entertaining and making me laugh on an evening when I was really nervous. Thank you too to Anna Jones, who came up with the idea of this competition.

The lovely people at Bloomsbury: the amazing Rebecca McNally, who has belief in my abilities as a writer. Which is incredible. My fantastic editor, Zöe Griffiths, who taught me how to get to the heart of the story and who was so kind and encouraging throughout. I look forward to holding your baby boy. Helen Vick, Hannah Sandford and Talya Baker for their meticulous editing and clever comments. And Rohan Eason for the beautiful illustrations that adorn these pages.

My friends: Susannah Garton, who stayed up all night in India to find out if I'd won. You were so excited, you are such a friend, you know me so well. Chris Cunningham, who bought me my first computer and told me to write. You promised to illustrate one of my books – don't forget that, Chriz. James Meeke – my spiritual advisor and my best male friend – you put up with a lot in terms of what you have to listen to, and you have so much faith in me. You make me laugh all the time and I love that we are on the same page. I hope we always will be. Your command of emoticons is really tiptop, dear, and improving all the time. Samantha Townsend – for all the HH and MH and every secret we share. Love our friendship. So happy you are there twenty-four hours a day (because you can't sleep either). Duncan Reavill – for the constancy of your friendship, for being prepared to discuss Nietzsche's aphorisms, and defining Rule 3 to someone who is no good at maths – that *is* a Fact. Polly Fulcher – you won't like my saying this, but you are so lovely and beautiful through and through. Leanne Galloway – chick! What if we'd never met? You are a wonderful friend and I'm so proud to have you in my life. Laura-Sue Rowe – for being so excited by this and so encouraging. Sarah Laws – for all those years of writing together, and the wonderful nights of food and laughter and honesty in your underground kitchen. Love you and Simon, Nancy and Hope. Lucy Onley and my god-daughter Emily. Roger Harris. Sam and Emily Jones. Natalia Conte – for those beautiful years in Rome.

The children I teach at Exeter Cathedral School. I love all of you. But I have to mention a few in particular: Celia Nowill, Emma Murphy, Lucy Fitzpatrick, Harry Fishwick, Francesca Vercoe, Florence Rihll, Lizzie Coldrick, Susannah Benson, Holly Thornton, Anna Hall and Rufus Stanier. Thank you for the surprise party, and the unicorn balloons. And all your love and support. Celia, thank you for being the first person to pre-order this book. What faith you have. I have avoided pathetic fallacy. To a certain extent. Although you will spot some. And I can only apologise for the exclamation marks.

All my friends at ECS. You are so kind. So good. So funny. So talented. Especially you, Jerry Jermyn and Martin Crocker, Sarah Butler Evans, the Penningtons, Nigel and Dana Bagnall, Lucy Lewis (and your shirt dresses), Jackie Lapraik, Mandy Bennett and the lovely T. Porter! Thank you also to my wonderful new Headmaster Mr James Featherstone who has already been so supportive of my writing career and promised me a 'do'.

All the gifted and talented children I teach at Exeter University, in particular Katie Brocksom, Lucja Kumala, Lyra Henderson and Kellan and Wolfgang Jollands.

And of course Cherry Dodwell who has encouraged me endlessly to be a writer over our ten years working at university together.

And finally all the children who will read this book. I do hope you like it, I really do. It would be pure magic if you did.